THE
RED GERANIUM

The Gift that Brings a Happy Future

HELEN HENDRICKS FRIESS

iUniverse LLC
Bloomington

KATIE

Katie Winston stood looking out the window of her law office on the twenty-seventh floor of the Newburg Building in Pittsburgh, Pennsylvania. She loved looking at the scene. It was a view of the headwaters of the Ohio River just after it was formed by the joining of the Monongehala and Allegheny Rivers that flowed from the mountains in central Pennsylvania. The river was not sparkling this afternoon as it did when the sun shone brightly on it. The clouds today were dark overhead and seemed to hint at a cold rain. The usual bright autumn colors of the trees were also subdued but Katie remembered the bright green leaves of summer, then the beautiful reds, rust, orange and yellow of the leaves that were now turning brown and gray. She loved looking at the river. She claimed the Ohio River as her own. For a moment she thought back to the first day she came to work at the law firm. She had been uneasy and a bit nervous. She hadn't felt for sure that she should be here. She wasn't even sure she wanted to be practicing law.

But during the year she had attained success well beyond her expectations. She smiled and shook her head. Who ever thought she would be where she was today? She had learned so much. She knew she loved the practice of law. She was happy to be at this firm in Pittsburgh.

Katie was small in stature but had a very big heart and felt she had found her calling in helping others. Her light brown hair with natural blonde highlights was always pulled back into a bun on the days she was in court. On non-court days her hair fell gently to her shoulders and framed her beautiful face and emphasized her big blue eyes. Many people misjudged her innocent appearance when facing her in court. At that time she became a passionate advocate for her clients, surprising her opponents with her intelligence and ability to get the facts from a witness.

She was the child of two consulting and teaching attorneys in Washington, D.C. They took occasional cases. The parents expected, or at least hoped, their children would follow in their footsteps. Her two older brothers loved law the way their parents did. Both graduated from law school and became very successful: one in New York and one on the West Coast. Now she was an attorney in Pittsburgh.

It had been a hard demanding year but she had learned so much. She reached out and touched the green leaves of the bright red geranium plant that sat on the window sill. Carl Wilson, who had been in this office and then moved to a larger one, had told Katie the geranium was a good-luck plant. He said it always brought good things to the person who owned it. He had great success while in this office. He was promoted to vice president and moved to a large corner office. When Carl gave the plant to Katie he told her he was sure the plant would also bring her good luck. Though skeptical, Katie graciously accepted the plant. Now she was beginning to believe it might have mystical powers. Her first year as a practicing attorney had certainly brought her success. Now she was moving to a new and challenging assignment. She was very happy she had accepted the offer to come here to Pittsburgh.

For a moment she allowed herself to remember the despair she felt during her final years of school in Washington, D.C. Most days she wanted to curl up into a ball and not leave her dorm room. Her family, though strong and loving, had set high standards for her to follow. Her courses had not seemed too difficult, not because she was brilliant, but probably because the subject of law was ordinary, common conversation at the dinner table while she was growing up. Katie decided she must have absorbed it all, because her studies presented few challenges. But school had not been a place where she formed the lifelong friends so many students do. She had made one very special, extremely special friend. And he became so much more. He had introduced Katie to a new world defined by the beauty of nature. Soon they were spending all their time together, identifying plants, learning about the stars, and visiting zoos and aquariums. He was a hard-working young man who loved his studies. He seemed very sincere about his feelings for her and she fell in love with him. She assumed she would be with this man for the rest of her life.

He was a member of the National Guard and as soon as he graduated he was sent to Iraq. The letters they wrote each other were full of love, passion and plans for a future together. One day the e-mails stopped coming. She continued to write and send messages to him. Then the final letter came, a Dear John letter. He didn't say he had met anyone new. He simply indicated Katie should find a new love and move on with her life. Katie thought her life was over. She went through the motions of living. She thought about him constantly, wondering if he had met someone new. Or maybe she had said something wrong. Her heart ached and she spent a lot of time curled up in a ball unable to get out of bed. Her parents never passed judgment on the man but encouraged her to finish her classes and begin a new life.

When she graduated from law school she was offered this position in Pittsburgh. Much to the chagrin of her parents, she asked for a six-month delay in starting her new position, and it was granted.

She used the money her grandparents left her to join some friends for a six month tour of Europe. Shortly after arriving in Paris, she and her friends were asked to join with a humanitarian group going to Africa to work with the displaced people there. These were people who were moving from one country to another seeking political refuge as well as food and a place to live.

Katie grew up quickly on that trip to Africa. She saw masses of people fleeing their homes and country, leaving behind the friends and the houses they had worked so hard to build. The people were weary and many were very sick. The refugee camps were crowded. There was sickness and despair everywhere. The people had left their home country with only the clothes on their backs. Fathers carried the toddlers on their shoulders while mothers nestled the babies in their arms. The people had very little hope; no reason to keep living. They had no food, no beds, and no shelter. Many of the people were suffering from disease and other illnesses. Katie had been shocked and sickened when she thought about the life she had lived in Washington, D.C. She sent e-mails home telling about the dire conditions. A friend of her father had read the letters and forwarded them on to the local newspaper which ran a series of the letters describing the living conditions of these people. The articles then were featured on a local TV show. After six months in Africa she returned home because she had made a commitment to the law firm in Pittsburgh. She had not been sure where she wanted to be. She had wondered if her calling was to work with refugees in Africa instead of practicing law.

She was very unsettled when she moved to Pittsburgh. But she knew she should fulfill the two-year commitment to the firm. The publicity of her articles had reached Pittsburgh and the people at the firm were very complimentary. They also told her that first-year employees at this firm usually prepare briefs and do research. Could she ever be satisfied doing that after working so closely with people? Her parents urged her to fulfill her commitment. After that, if she wanted to go back to Africa to work as a humanitarian, they would support her choice.

After a couple of weeks doing routine look-ups, a

senior attorney of the firm, Richard Jenner, called her to his office.

He told her about some family friends, a couple in their eighties, who had apparently run into very difficult times. Mr. Jenner had always thought the couple was comfortable financially, but he learned they had lost their home in foreclosure. Since Katie seemed to have an affinity for people, he asked her to look into the situation and report back to him. Mr. Jenner told her he had called the couple to tell them he would try to see if they could recover any of their funds. He wondered if perhaps the necessary paperwork for their insurance or Medicare had been accurate.

Katie went to their home, which was a small apartment in the upstairs of an old house in a rundown seedy part of the city. Bonnie and Paul welcomed her graciously with old-world charm and apologized for their humble surroundings. They were both small in stature but carried their bodies with an air of dignity. Bonnie's dress was out of style but Katie recognized the designer of the well-made garment. Paul was wearing a white shirt and tie under a sweater. They walked slowly and carefully but with a touch of class. Their three rooms were small and crowded with furniture that was very oversized for the rooms. Bonnie insisted on serving her tea while Paul brought out boxes of bills, receipts and business papers. Katie suggested they sit at the kitchen table so she had space to look at the papers.

"Tell me about your illness," Katie asked Bonnie. "You

look like you have made a full recovery. You are walking well and you look very young and beautiful."

"Thank you for the compliment. It helps me to feel young after quite a disastrous couple of years. I do believe I might not be here today had I continued with that terrible clinic," Bonnie said.

"Tell me about it."

"I began to have serious back problems. There was a spine clinic in our neighborhood that we could walk to for treatment. They told me treatment would take six months or more. I tried to be cooperative. But I kept getting worse. They said they were trying different methods to help me."

Paul continued the story. "We kept saying we felt we should try different treatments or see another doctor, but I guess we fell for their old lines. By this time we had used up the benefits from Medicare and our supplementary insurance. This stack of papers here will support what I have told you," he said as he handed her a bundle of papers. "When we told them we were out of money for treatments the manager referred us to a loan agency that would finance a mortgage on our house. We had lived in that house for almost sixty years. We lost our home soon after and moved here. By that time we had sold almost everything of any value to get money to live on."

Bonnie spoke, "Paul began to get very sick with worry about it all. We were getting deeper and deeper in debt. Every day more and more bills came in for this treatment or that. And I was getting worse all the time. Then Paul got pneumonia. I finally called EMS and they rushed him to a local hospital. While receiving treatment he told one of the doctors about my condition. We were referred to a doctor at that hospital who was able to identify a disc problem, which the doctors were able to fix. But we were left with mountains of bills and a very small pension to live on. Our savings were gone by that time," she said softly. "But we still have each other and have found we can scrape by."

"This is not the kind of life we planned for so carefully, but like she said, we do still have each other," Paul said quietly as he reached out to take Bonnie's hand.

Katie took their papers, gave them both a hug, and said she'd be in touch.

Katie studied all the medical records, did some research and found the clinic had bilked the couple, their insurance company and Medicare out of thousands of dollars. When their savings disappeared, the couple had mortgaged their home for money to live on. This mortgage bank charged them an illegal and very high rate of interest. With their limited income they could not meet the monthly payments. They sold many antiques and works of art to pay their living expenses. But now they had no resources left.

Katie was furious that this had happened in her own country. By the time she reported back to Mr. Jenner about the condition of his friends she had a folder full of evidence against the clinic and the mortgage bank. She documented everything and referenced the laws that supported her claims. She had prepared the necessary briefs to file with the courts.

Mr. Jenner was very surprised at the investigation and follow-up work Katie had done. He arranged for Katie to have her own small office so she would have more working space than she had in the company library. He said he would review her work. A short time later he called Katie into his office and told her to file the papers. Because of the dire conditions of the couple he got the proceedings moved to the front of the court docket.

He kept Katie by his side as the case proceeded through the system. When they went to trial he told Katie to present the case. He said he would be by her side. This was almost unheard of for a first-year attorney at that firm, but Katie really cared for the elderly couple and was passionate about helping them. When the rulings came down, the authorities were also involved. The health clinic and the mortgage bank were both closed. The monetary award was large and the couple was able to move to a very nice retirement community. Needless to say, Katie became a star at the firm and was given a larger office. The office she had moved into was the one she was now leaving: the office where she was given the lucky red geranium.

As she stood by the window that last day looking around the room, her thoughts were interrupted when her co-worker walked in the door carrying a large box.

"Sorry, Katie, I thought you had already gone," Greg Rossman said. "This is to be my new office."

"It's OK, Greg," she told him. "I just have a few things left to take home."

"I guess congratulations are in order for you," he said, a hint of envy in his voice. "I guess you're headed for the big times now."

"Not really, Greg," she said with a laugh. "And I

expect to be back here in a year to claim this office with the beautiful view."

"When are you leaving?" he asked.

"Tomorrow morning. I'll be meeting some members of the committee at UN Headquarters in New York and we'll be given our assignments. Then we'll be flown to some area of the world."

"And I suppose you speak every language in the world," he said with a sneer.

"I'm not doing this by myself. I'll be met by U.N. representatives who will be with me." Then, because she was tired of his nastiness she turned to him and said, "But I do speak three other languages. Please don't worry about me," she added in a soft kind voice. "I'll be fine."

With a touch of sarcasm he replied, "Well, you'll be the big important lady around here from now on. I guess it's because of your famous parents that you were asked to do this project."

"I love and respect and owe a lot to my parents, but I think I received this offer to serve with the U.N. because I worked hard to learn about the problems. I have seen first hand housing concerns both in Africa and the United States. It's a sad situation that should concern us all. Everyone deserves a home. I was very surprised when this firm encouraged me to accept the offer from the U.N. for a year. Everyone has been so kind and encouraging," she added, emphasizing the word "everyone."

Katie moved to the window and removed the red geranium. She placed it on the desk in front of Greg. "Carl Wilson had this office before me. Someone had given him this red geranium and told him it would bring him success. He received a promotion and a bigger office. I was skeptical about such a claim, but now I can believe it. I won't have any office for a year, but I'll get the opportunity to try to help people all over the world have a home. I'm giving this geranium to you with my best wishes for your success." Katie placed the plant on the desk in front of him.

"I don't believe in all that nonsense. Just throw it in the waste basket," Greg told her.

Katie was aghast. She loved this plant. But quietly she said, "I'll take it with me."

She took the box with her remaining personal items and the plant and left the room.

Maybe I am learning about maturity, she thought. *At least I didn't hit him. How can he be so cruel? This plant is magic.*

Driving back to her apartment she did begin to wonder what she would do with the geranium. She couldn't take it with her. She wasn't sure just what type of project she was to be assigned or where she would be working. The officials had indicated it had something to do with the U.N. Human Settlement Program, which estimates that as many as six billion people, or two-thirds of everyone on the planet, will be living in towns and cities by the year of 2050. Her research was expected to take a year. Then she would come back to Pittsburgh.

The night was chilly and damp so she was glad to arrive home. As she entered her apartment she placed the geranium on the kitchen counter. She finished packing the one bag that she would take with her. She looked around

there are homeless people everywhere; in Pittsburgh and all over the world. Katie hoped she could become one of the people who could provide help to them.

Katie returned to her apartment, packed a few more things, and then went to bed. Very early tomorrow morning she would fly to New York to meet with other members of the committee and begin a new phase of her life.

CHAPTER 2
BRYAN

The man lay huddled in a ball near the entrance of his "cave". He knew it was only a spot to hide from the rain but this underpass provided a home for him and a few other people. He had chosen to sleep nearest to the entrance. He always felt choked up when he was in tight, confined places. Most often he would drift off to sleep easily but as he lay there with his back to the wind and icy rain, which was falling more heavily now, the ground seemed unusually hard and damp. He couldn't remember the last time he had slept in a real bed or even on a cot. At the shelters the cots were placed close together. Sometimes he felt like he could not get his breath. He almost preferred sleeping on the open ground. But the icy rain kept him from the open fields tonight. He was glad he had some shelter. He tried to doze a little.

When he turned his body over to get a more comfortable position, his arm hit something. *What is that? Maybe a dog that needed some comfort? No, it was hard and stiff.* He sat up straight and in the light of the cars passing by he saw it was a box. He must have been sleeping deeper than he thought for he had neither heard nor felt anyone approach him.

Looking into the box he found food: sandwiches, fruit, (which he hadn't seen for months) cookies, and could it be…? Yes, it was a thermos bottle. Oh, how he hoped it had some hot coffee. He could see the other four people who were taking refuge start to stir. He grabbed the thermos and hid it in his coat pocket. He woke the others. As the wind howled around them they sat close to each other eating the sandwiches. They drank toasts to each other with their water bottles. As their hunger pains eased they noticed the red geranium.

"What's that?" one of them asked.

"That's a red geranium, stupid," another answered. "My grandmother always had them in her window box."

"Well, if you can't eat it, I'm not interested in it," another said.

The man who had found the box said, "It's a *Pelargonium Graveolens.*"

"Well, well, listen to Professor Bryan, La-di-dah."

They finished their sandwiches and went back to sleep.

Bryan didn't take offense at their mocking. But he couldn't go back to sleep either. He reached into his coat and pulled out the thermos of coffee, opened it, took a big gulp which nearly burned his mouth, put the lid back on and hid the thermos again. It seemed like it had been years since he had a cup of really hot coffee. *I'll share my food but I will not share this coffee. This is mine*, he thought.

Bryan was not able to go back to sleep. He began to think about his grandmother. Maybe it was the red geranium. His grandmother had beautiful flower gardens all around her house and yard and his job was to help her keep the gardens weeded. By the time he was five years old he knew the Latin name for each flower. Grandma told him it was just as easy to learn the Latin name as the common name. So he learned both names for each plant.

He hadn't thought about his grandmother for a long time. He missed her constant encouragement and the way she pushed him to succeed. Succeed?? What's success? When he learned his Grandma had died he felt like a part of him died with her. She had been the only mother he had known. He really missed her; still, he would not have wanted her to see him today. Now he was a homeless recluse with no home, no job, no friends and no hope for the future. He had become a street person. One who had not had a bath or shower for some weeks, he realized.

Was it really fair for him to blame his condition on his service with the Army in Iraq? Probably not. But the bad dreams of seeing the body parts of his new friends and hearing their cries and the sounds of explosions were memories that haunted him. If he'd been able get his head on straight he probably could have still had a good life. The dreams stayed with him. They would not go away. Bryan lay on the cold, damp ground, restless, unable to get back to sleep. For the first time in many months he began to wonder why he was settling for this kind of life. Could he do better? Or would it end up with another stint in the VA hospital and then back to the streets? Is this really the way he wanted to live his life? As bad as his conditions were, was it easier to live with them than to try to find another way? He began to develop a headache. He hoped his old troubles were not coming back. There was nothing else he could do anyway. It was a cold, rainy night. He was better off staying in the shelter of the highway overhead. He had no where else to go.

He lay there tossing and turning. But as he did so he touched the red geranium which again made him think of his grandmother. He would be so ashamed if she saw him giving up on life. Finally, unable to get back to sleep, he got up. He placed the thermos of coffee back in his coat pocket. He picked up the red geranium and left the area. He didn't know where he would go or what he was doing. But, by moving he was taking the first step. He saw a vision in his mind of his grandmother smiling.

He started to walk along the highway. The rain was coming down a lot harder now but he didn't notice. He would go where the road took him.

As he walked he was oblivious to the light traffic passing by him in the darkness of the night. A driver of a semi-rig stopped beside him and asked him if he wanted a ride.

The driver asked him, "Where are you going?"

Bryan said, "I don't know."

The driver said, "Well, I can take you twenty miles on your road to nowhere. It's not every day I see a homeless man carrying a red geranium walking along the road in the middle of the night."

The next couple of days Bryan's journey took him into the mountain area and through many small towns and farmers' fields. When he got too tired to go on, he would look for a doorway or some type of shelter. He looked in the trash cans for some bit of garbage to eat. He found very little. Then he moved on. For three days he traveled alone, sometimes getting a ride for a few miles. Since he didn't know where he was headed, how would he know when he got there? He still carried the thermos bottle; he wasn't sure why since the coffee had been gone before noon of his first day on the road. By the third day, he knew he needed food.

As he continued walking he was offered a ride by another man driving a semi who asked him, "When did you last eat?"

"Not for a while," Bryan told him.

"Here's an energy bar," the man said handing it to Bryan. "About ten miles up ahead is a big family owned supermarket. If you go in and ask for Pete, he's the owner, I know for sure he'll let you trade something for some food."

"I have nothing to trade," Bryan said.

"You have that red geranium. Pete's a good man. You'll get a sandwich. Tell him Einstein sent you."

When they arrived at the supermarket, Bryan made his way toward the entrance. He caught a reflection of himself in the store window. He looked old, dirty, and dangerous. And silly. What grown man goes into a store trying to trade a geranium for food? Yet he really didn't want to let go of the plant. It seemed like a bit of home was with him. But if he didn't eat, he knew he would be lying on the side of the road somewhere. He swallowed hard and pushed the door open.

There was a row of check-out registers along the front of the store. He saw a man about fifty or sixty years of age talking to one of the cashiers. He was about the same height as Bryan but probably weighed about a hundred pounds more. His hair was thin on top He approached the man.

"Excuse me, please, are you Pete?" he asked the man.

"Yes. Who are you?" the man asked in a kind voice.

"My name is Bryan. A man named Einstein gave me a ride and said you might trade me a sandwich for this red geranium."

Pete took the red geranium, turned it around slowly and looked it over. "I think we can make a deal. Come this way with me." As they walked to Pete's office they passed through the deli section where Pete told Bryan to pick up a pre-packaged sandwich. Pete took him to the office where he poured a cup of coffee for Bryan and indicated that Bryan should eat.

"Do you have a story you'd like to talk about?" Pete asked him.

Bryan looked down at his feet and said, "Thank you very much for the gift of this sandwich and coffee."

Pete only said "Uh-huh." Then he added, "Where did you come from?"

"Most recently, Pittsburgh, but my home used to be on the East Coast."

"Got a place to sleep tonight?"

"I'll find something."

"Not in our little town. Come with me. We'll go to my house."

"I can't go to your home."

"My wife will be very happy to have you come home with me. She's made vegetable soup and an apple pie for dinner. She makes the best pies in the world. Come on, let's go home. Would you mind carrying the red geranium for me? I think she'll like it."

Bryan was never sure why he so calmly let himself be ordered around. *What has come over me*, he wondered. *I'm filthy dirty and I smell like a bad sewer. I can't do this.*

"You're being very kind to me but I can't enter your home. I'm much too dirty. Please drop me off at the next crossroads and I'll continue on my way."

"Well, maybe you'd like a hot shower and a change of clothes first. Would that make you feel better?" Pete asked as he pulled into the driveway of his home.

Darkness had already started to fall and Bryan really didn't know what to do. "You obviously know I can't pay you for what you're doing for me."

"Maybe you'll bring a smile to my Jeannie's face. We lost our only son in Iraq and our home has been sad and gloomy. My Jeannie needs someone to fuss over. Please let her pamper you. It will be good to see a smile on her face. I'll ask nothing more from you."

What love this man has for his wife, that he would bring

a dirty stranger into her home to try to cheer her up, Bryan thought. *Apparently their son had died while in Iraq.*

"I'll try my best," Bryan told Pete.

"Brought home company," Pete called out as they entered the door.

If Jeannie was surprised or disappointed she never let it show. "Welcome to our home," she said quietly, as she reached out to shake hands with Bryan.

For the first time in more than a year Bryan was embarrassed by his appearance. "I'm much to dirty to be in your home. I must be on my way."

"There's nothing wrong with you that a little soap and water won't fix," Jeannie told him. Then turning to Pete she said "Take Bryan up to Joe's room. You should find soap and shampoo in the bathroom," she quietly told him. "Our Joe was about the same size as you. Find some clean clothes and then come down to supper. The pie has fifteen more minutes in the oven. We can eat together after you've had a chance to clean up."

Pete took him to Joe's room. Pete opened dresser drawers and the closet and told Bryan to help himself. Then he left the room.

Bryan saw pictures on the wall of a young man from childhood thru prom dates and finally his official Army picture. Bryan felt pangs of guilt as if he was intruding yet he had to be honest. The thought of a shower with hot water was something he only had when he was in the VA hospital. On the streets even cold showers were few and far between.

He headed for the bathroom. It was clean and white

with big thirsty towels waiting to be used. There was shampoo and soap and toothbrushes and toothpaste. There were razors and shaving creams. He looked into the mirror. He did not recognize himself. Bryan looked at his long shaggy hair and beard. At one time his hair had been blonde but he could see only grimy dirt there now. He looked again into the mirror as he undressed and saw a naked body he did not recognize. It was all skin and bones. He used to keep his weight at just under two hundred pounds on a six-foot frame. Now he looked like he was much shorter and weighed around one hundred thirty pounds. It was the first good look Bryan had of his body in two or more years. As he washed under the shower of hot water he felt bones protruding all over his body. He remembered when his body was firm and fit. His arms looked like two sticks by his side. He felt as if it would take forever to get the grime off. He found underwear and sox in the drawer and noticed that Pete had pulled both sneakers and loafers from the closet for Bryan. He found a pair of jeans and a sweat shirt. As he combed his hair as a finishing touch he looked in the mirror again. He shook his head at his image and went to the kitchen.

"Now you look better," Jeannie said as he came into the room. "I thought it would be cozier to eat here in the kitchen tonight. I hope you like my soup. I put everything but the kitchen sink into it," she said with a smile, as she ladled soup into a bowl and placed it before him.

Bryan honestly told her the soup was the best he had ever eaten and after almost three bowls of it, Jeannie began to believe him. The apple pie truly was the best in the world.

Jeannie had put the red geranium on the end of the kitchen table. "That's a beautiful plant. There must be a story connected to it since you apparently carried it for a long way."

"Yes, ma'am. I carried it all the way from Pittsburgh." Bryan became very quiet and bowed his head slightly. "Even though I know you can tell it from my appearance, I have been living on the streets for some time. A few nights ago as I slept in an underpass I was awakened when my hand touched something. Someone had come to the location and left a box of sandwiches. Next to the box sat this red geranium. I woke the others who were sleeping there and we shared the sandwiches and fruit. But I could not take my eyes off the geranium. It made me remember my grandmother. I couldn't get back to sleep. I kept remembering Grandma. She provided a home for me for many years. She taught me so much, including all about flowers and plants. She always had many red geraniums around the house in the summer. She had very high hopes that I would find a future working or teaching about flowers. As I lay on the cold, damp ground I couldn't help but think of how I was letting my grandmother down. She was a proud, hard-working woman. She was tough with her discipline but it was always done in a loving way. I tried to sleep but I kept hearing her tell me I needed to get busy and improve my life. I felt like I was in a daze as I picked up the plant and left the shelter of the underpass and started to walk. I was walking away but I didn't know where I was going. And I seem to have stopped when a man named Einstein told me to ask Pete for a sandwich."

"I think your grandmother was speaking to you through the geranium. She wants you to have a good life," Jeannie said. "She must have been a very good woman. Did she raise you?"

"Yes. My parents both died in an accident when I was very young and I moved in with Grandma. She was a very special lady. I never heard her say anything bad about anyone, but she would get very impatient with someone who did wrong. She lived every day as best and as fully as she could. She tried not to let any wasted days get by her." Bryan paused, deep in thought. "She wasn't very happy when I joined the National Guard, but it was a way to help pay college expenses. At the time I never expected to end up in Iraq. She died while I was over there. I wasn't able to be with her at the end of her life. But I remember she told me her spirit would always be with me."

"Maybe your grandmother brought you here to our door," Pete said as he looked at his wife.

"You had a son," Bryan said. "It must make you feel sad to see me in his clothes."

Jeannie ignored his comment and reached out and laid her hand over his. "Pete's right. Maybe your grandmother brought you to us because we, or maybe I should say I, need to try to start living again. Joe was a vibrant happy young man who loved life. He wouldn't have wanted me to stop living. Seeing you in his old sweatshirt makes me remember many happy times."

"I think this is the first time I have had on clean clothes

for more than a month. I can't even remember the last time I changed clothes. I got the clothes I was wearing at one of the shelters. You have been so kind to me. You must feel sad to see me wearing your son's clothes," he repeated again shaking his head. "You must have many questions for me. I will be happy to answer them and then I'll be on my way again. I will never forget your kindness. I feel stronger than I have felt for many months."

"We're glad if we can help," Pete said.

"You can't leave tonight," Jeannie said. "Let us help you as you start your new life."

"No, no, I must leave. I've been told I sometimes cry out in my sleep. I can't stay here."

"Son," Pete said quietly, "maybe you won't cry out in your sleep anymore now that you have decided to move on with your life. Stay and give it a try."

"You know I have no money to pay you for what you're doing for me."

"Then you'll have to come to work with me tomorrow. A day's wage for food and lodging. How does that sound? We'll leave for the store around seven or so."

"I'll do it but I know nothing about grocery stores."

"Then I'll teach you. You can stock shelves, bag groceries, sweep the floors; there are many things you can do."

Bryan sat quietly with his head in his hands. He felt as if he was at a crossroads. "What if I can't do the work?" he asked quietly.

"Then we'll teach you. Now that everything is settled, let's clear the table and do the dishes," Pete said.

Jeannie spoke. "Let me help you choose some

appropriate shirts to wear to work. The jeans will be fine and you'll be given a big white apron to wear. Pete insists on it. He wants everyone to look somewhat alike."

"I bet Pete doesn't favor long hair," Bryan said.

"That's true," Pete said with a smile.

"If you have a pair of scissors I'll cut it off," Bryan told him.

"Nonsense," Jeannie said. "Come with me. Pete can do the dishes."

"Get out of here," Pete said in a gruff, yet loving manner.

Jeannie reached for a set of keys hanging by the back door. "Come with me," she told Bryan.

Together they left the house and walked along a garden path to a building that looked like a small house: a smaller version of the main house. Once inside, Bryan saw it was a hair salon.

Inside the door Jeannie turned on the lights, stopped, looked around and then reached out to hold on to Bryan.

"This is the first time I've been here since we got the word that Joe was dead. I had a good business before that but somehow I just could never come back in here. Just like your life stopped for you, I felt like my life was over. Maybe we can help each other."

"My visit is upsetting your life. I should move on."

"Or maybe your visit is going to give me back my life," Jeannie said as she looked at Bryan with tears in her eyes. "Let's both work on it." She reached out for a cape to put over Bryan's shoulders. "Don't be too critical of me if I snip your ear by mistake. How short can I cut it?" she asked as she began to cut his hair.

"You're the hair stylist. You make the decision."

Jeannie began to snip away.

"You have a lot of natural curl. We'll leave it just long enough for everyone to see some of it."

Bryan was very surprised when he looked in the mirror. "This hair cut makes me feel like a new person. You sure know your business," Bryan told her as he looked in the mirror. "You have a real talent for making someone like me look so good," he added with a smile.

"I used to be quite successful. Maybe I will open the shop again," Jeannie said quietly.

"Do I pass your inspection, Pete?" Bryan asked when they returned to the house.

"You pass it one thousand percent," Pete answered as he reached out to take his wife in his arms. "Welcome home, my darling," he told his wife as he held her tightly. "I've missed you."

Bryan felt very excited as he got into some clean pajamas which were laid on the turned-back covers of the bed. He couldn't remember when he had last slept in a bed. He thought about the journey that had brought him here. There must have been magic in that red geranium. For the first time in many years he thought of the simple childhood prayer that his grandmother had taught him – *Watch me safely through the night* – but he was asleep before he could finish the prayer. He slept soundly for the first time in years. When he awakened he realized that it was nearly noon. He quickly got out of bed, treated himself to a quick shower, got dressed and made his way to the sun-lit kitchen.

Jeannie was taking chocolate chip cookies from the oven. The smell of the melting chocolate filled the air. She greeted him with a big smile. "Well, sleepyhead, I'm glad to see you up and moving. Sit right here and I'll fix you a big omelet." She poured him a cup of hot coffee and then set a pitcher of orange juice on the table indicating he should help himself.

"What kind of toast would you like? Check out the loaves on the counter."

"Ma'am, anything you fix would be wonderful. I apologize for sleeping so late. I was supposed to go to work with Pete this morning."

"Pete thought maybe you needed today to rest up after your journey. Were you able to get to sleep without too much trouble?" she asked.

"Truthfully, I remember getting into bed. It has been so long since I have slept in a real bed. I just laid there for a minute or so enjoying the feel of sheets under me and a soft blanket over me. But I remember nothing else until I woke up about fifteen minutes ago. I hope my being here didn't upset your schedule."

"I haven't kept a schedule since we heard of Joe's death. I guess I have not been able to accept the fact that he is gone. Your coming here has made me realize that I'm certainly not the only person in the world who suffered a loss in the war. Maybe we can be friends who can help each other."

"I'd consider it an honor to be called your friend," Bryan said quietly.

"I think your grandmother raised a good man. She would be proud to see you make this new start."

"Would you suggest that I go to the market now? Though I certainly appreciate the long sleep I had, I do want to pay for my keep," Bryan told her.

"Tomorrow will be soon enough unless you feel you must move on."

"I think it's time I stop running away."

"I agree," Jeannie said with a smile. "Then come with me. I want to go back into my hair salon. I'd appreciate having someone with me for this second trip in there."

"I'll be right beside you." As Bryan said the words he realized that it was the first time in years that he was doing something for someone instead of asking for something for himself. It made him feel good.

Together they walked to the shop. The room seemed warm and cozy with the bright noon sun coming in the front windows. There were two styling chairs and two shampoo bowls. The shelves were lined with shampoo bottles and hair care items. The chairs were covered with sheets and the air in the room was stale and heavy. Bryan tried not to notice the dust on the floor and cobwebs on the lights.

Bryan looked into the big mirror. "I must say I really like the haircut you gave me. I look presentable – well almost presentable -- for the first time in two or three years."

"I think you look great. You just need to put some meat on your bones."

"I didn't realize until last night how much weight I have lost. But after your delicious dinner and that big breakfast, I feel almost fat," he told her.

Jeannie started to laugh. Her cell phone rang. She answered in the midst of her laughter.

Bryan also smiled as he listened to her conversation with Pete.

"Yes, I was laughing."

"Yes, it feels good."

"Yes, he slept until noon and now we are in the shop. I'm going to get his opinion about a remodel or at least a new coat of paint so I can reopen it."

"I love you too, Pete. Goodbye."

Bryan saw a look of love and softness on her face as she ended her call. He almost felt he was intruding on a private moment so he busied himself looking into corners and under sinks.

"I don't know much about a beauty shop, but you look like you have a good set-up here. Do you really need to change anything?"

"Maybe I just need someone to tell me I have the strength to do it."

"Let me be that person," Bryan said. "You have the strength to do it." He paused and then went on. "And I have the strength to change, thanks to the chance that you and Pete took on me. I will change my life. I will work hard to become a stronger person."

Jeannie reached out and put her arms around him. "Maybe we needed each other."

The next morning Bryan was up and waiting for Pete to leave for work. Bryan had many concerns: was he dressed appropriately, was he going to be able to do the work, would he be able to react in a civil manner to the world around him. Pete and Jeannie both reassured him that he could do it as they left the house.

"You got a driver's license?" Pete asked Bryan as he drove to the store.

"Yes, it's the one piece of ID I held on to," he said reaching into his pocket to produce it. "I need it to get into the VA hospital."

"Did you spend a lot of time there?" Pete asked.

"Well, I'd go admit myself when I was desperate or the police would take me. They'd pump me full of meds and then send me on my way. My job in Iraq was to locate and disarm roadside bombs. I made it home when most of my different crews did not. I have been unable to shake the memories. I seem to live with the flashbacks of the horror. The meds I received at the hospital would help for a time and then they seemed to make me worse. I finally decided not to go back to the hospital. But I couldn't seem to function without medication. I felt I was in a Catch-22 situation. I have been unable to sleep without nightmares. But I did sleep well these last two nights for the first time in years. You and your wife have been very kind to me. I hope I don't let you down."

"Well, I'm sure you'll learn quickly. Let me tell you about a special customer. Her name is Alma. I think she is in her eighties. She lives high on the top of the mountain. Summer or winter she walks down a mountain trail about twice a week to buy a few groceries. I try to be certain that I or someone in the store drive her home. She is a very proud lady so we tell her we have an errand to do out her way and will be glad to drop her off at her home. I hope you will be alert to help her. I think she must be lonely for company for she rarely buys enough food for more than a day or so at a time."

"Do you have some special job for me today?" Bryan asked.

"Jon Webster manages the store for me. He'll give you an assignment till you learn the ropes."

The men walked into the store together just before opening. Pete made an announcement on the PA system that Bryan was now an employee at the store and would be learning everything from the ground up so everyone should help him. There were brief greetings of "Hi Bryan," or "Hello," or "Welcome," and then everyone got back to their job. Bryan had worried that they might recognize him as the derelict drifter who had come into the store two days earlier. But no one seemed to pay any extra attention to him.

The first day Jon gave Bryan a variety of chores: helping unload boxes from delivery trucks; helping to re-stock the shelves by removing all the merchandise, dusting, placing the new supplies in the back and checking expiration dates on the older supplies before placing them in the front. He swept some floors when merchandise was dropped or spilt. There was a small room with a few tables and chairs where a customer could sit and eat the salad or sandwich he or she had purchased at the deli section. Bryan was told to keep the room clean, the tables wiped off and supplied with napkins, straws, etc. He was called to help bag groceries a few times.

"Everyone treat you OK today?" Pete asked Bryan when they started for home that first night.

"Everyone was very kind to me. Everyone seems so kind to each other," Bryan told him.

"You know something Bryan, even if you had not lifted a finger today I owe you big time for what you did for my Jeannie. She has been going through the motions of living since Joe was killed. But when you let her cut your hair, it seemed to awaken in her the desire to open her shop again. I owe you for bringing her out of her fallen spirits. I told Jeannie last night that maybe there is magic in that red geranium. It helped you reconnect with your grandmother who will keep you on the right path and it is helping Jeannie and me reconnect with the world."

Bryan and Pete both could see that Jeannie seemed to have a new energy when they arrived home.

"And how did everything go?" she asked Bryan.

"Everyone was wonderful. They were so helpful. But I can't impose on you and Pete again tonight."

"Plan to stay for a few days. You'll get a paycheck on Saturday, then you can decide if you need to go on your way again or if you want to try our town for a while. I think Jeannie and I both need company."

"Did the day seem like it would never end?" Jeannie asked.

"The day went by very quickly. The grocery business is fascinating. I had no idea there were so many different parts to it," Bryan told her. Then turning to Pete he asked, "How long have you owned the store?"

"My dad opened it as a mom-and-pop kind of store with bread and milk and little else. I took over the store when I came back from Vietnam."

"You are a highly respected man at the store," Bryan told him.

"That's because he is such a good man," Jeannie said as she gave him a hug.

There was a section of the store that kept drawing Bryan to it. It was the section of the store where fresh cut flowers were sold along with a few house plants. Bryan was told the space had been rented to a florist from a nearby town. The flowers were neglected between visits by the florist's rep. During Bryan's first week the section seemed to be calling to him. Maybe having had the red geranium had re-awakened in Bryan his childhood dream of having his own business. He had always thought about a landscaping business. Or maybe any business having something to do with flowers or plants. Or maybe even teaching about them. He remembered how he enjoyed his botany classes at the university. Did he dare to dream that someday he might own his own shop?

Bryan's life settled into a new routine over the next couple of weeks. He continued to live with Pete and Jeannie, joining them for church on Sunday and watching the football games on Sunday afternoon. But Bryan knew it was time for him to take another step.

So far he had collected two paychecks, and while they were just slightly above minimum wage, he was not paying for food or shelter. Could he learn to live on those earnings? How would he get to work? He had no car. What would his grandmother tell him to do? Thinking about her always gave him comfort. As he sat having coffee and thinking about his life, he suddenly remembered that he was not as broke as he thought he was. His VA disability pension checks and the money from the sale of his grandmother's house were in a bank account in Maine. *I do have some money,* he thought. Then he had a second thought. *If I start to spend that money will I drift back into my old life. I must, and will, learn to live on what I make here. I will give myself six months. If I don't backslide into my old life style I will then consider how I should live my life.*

The next day at lunch time Bryan put on his coat and said he was going for a walk. He was pretty certain that he had seen a small residential motel not too far from the store. He wanted to be able to walk to work. He passed by a gym with a sign that said it was open from 5 a.m. to midnight. There was a diner on one corner. He made his way to the motel where he found the rates were low enough for him to manage on his take-home pay. The small kitchenette would work well as a kitchen. He needed no more space than that, at least not now. *If I can make it on my own for six months, then I will plan a future,* he repeated over and over to himself.

It seemed to take no time at all for Pete, Jeannie and Bryan to become a family. But Bryan knew the time had come for him to tell them it was time he moved out of their home.

"Oh, no," Jeannie cried. "Are we doing something wrong?"

"No, Jeannie, you've done everything right. You and Pete have given me a home, a family, and a job. Most of all you helped me believe in myself. But I must not allow myself to be dependent on you. And I'd like your help to become independent. I admit I'm a bit frightened to take the next step by myself. I hope you will help me. I have found a place to live on my own. It's in the old motel units over on Center Street. There is a kitchenette unit available. If you let me keep my job, Pete, it's a place I can afford. I have to prove to myself that I can do this. I can walk to work from there. I've also been thinking ahead. I have money in the bank on the east coast. My VA disability pension plus the money from the sale of my grandmother's house is on deposit there. I have taken no money out. I guess I forgot it was there. I don't want to touch it until I have proven I can take care of myself on any amount of money I earn. You have been so kind to me. I guess I'm asking you if we can continue to be friends. Can I come to you for advice? Will you help me to stay stable and healthy?"

Pete walked over to the chair where Bryan was sitting.

"Stand up, Bryan."

Bryan stood.

Pete embraced him in a bear hug and Jeannie soon joined them.

"We'll be here for you."

"I have another favor to ask of you, Pete."

"Go ahead."

"I have noticed that you have a small section in the store set aside for flowers and plants. I mean no offense but I think it is neglected. I know the flowers are brought in on consignment by an outside outfit. Would you mind if I spend my own time there taking care of the plants? I've noticed there is not a real flower shop in town and I think there is a market for one. I've noticed that many restaurants and shops rent potted plants to decorate their areas. They all look pretty sad. Maybe in time, after I prove I can stay stable, I can take my money and open up a plant rental and flower shop. Your help would give me a chance to see if it's doable."

"You can become a plant doctor," Jeannie said with a big smile on her face.

"Well, I have to prove to myself I can be stable for at least six months," he repeated.

Pete spoke. "You can take over management of the flower shop. You can do anything you like with it. If it starts to make a profit you can claim all the rewards."

That night Bryan stopped by the gym that was close to his new home and asked if he could get a part-time job there in exchange for using the equipment. The owner was surprised by the request but told him he could come in at five every morning and mop all the floors. In exchange for pay he could use any of the equipment any time he wanted to do so.

As Bryan began to work out regularly he felt his muscles start to waken. He was eating regularly and had already gained weight. In just a couple of weeks he could see a few results of his new exercise routine.

Even though Bryan was living in one room, working two jobs, one at minimum wage and the other for no wage, he felt like a king. He was now taking care of himself. He was not dependent on strangers for hand-outs. He had a real bed to sleep in each night. He occasionally had flashback dreams of his days in Iraq but he was able to recognize them as dreams and go back to sleep. More often he had pleasant dreams: his grandmother tucking him into bed at night in the small bedroom off the kitchen where he slept or climbing into her big bed to hear her read a favorite story or maybe just tell him tales about his mother and father.

His parents had died in a small plane crash when he was only three years old. The family had been flying from Washington, D.C. to Maine to visit Grandmother. Bryan had survived the crash. Grandma ran a Bed and Breakfast inn in a small coastal village. From early spring to late fall, the inn was very busy. Grandma hired a handyman to come each day to take care of the building and yard. Bryan followed the man around who taught him many skills. Grandma taught him about flowers and trees as well as how to become a good man. The old house always needed repairs. Money from the room rentals was adequate but not plentiful. But Bryan was surrounded by an abundance of love.

And though he unconsciously always sought the approval of his grandmother, Bryan now had friends and family. He had Pete and Jeannie. He knew he would forever be in their debt.

CHAPTER 3
PETE AND JEANNIE

The night that Bryan left their house to sleep in his new home was a sad, lonely night for Pete and Jeannie.

"I didn't realize how much I would miss him," Jeannie told Pete as they got ready for bed.

"Neither did I," Pete answered. "Isn't it strange how quickly he seemed to settle in here."

"It's not so strange when you have magic working for you," Jeannie said with a smile as she turned the pot of the red geranium. "This makes me remember the red geraniums my parents planted each summer along the walk to the front porch. I swear, Pete, I'm almost beginning to believe in the power of this plant."

"I know what you mean. My first thought when I saw it was remembering the window boxes at my childhood home. Dad and Mom always planted geraniums. When I first saw Bryan I wanted to hold my nose and run away, but there was something about the way he protected the plant that soon changed the picture of him. Instead of the dirt and grime I saw the eyes of a truly desperate man with one worldly possession: a potted plant. Everything after that just seemed to happen. I gave him a sandwich and brought him home. I didn't even call to ask if it was OK. I just did it."

"How do you do it, Pete? You always know what I need before I even know it. I know you brought him home because you thought maybe it would help me. It might make me forget my grief for a little while. And it did. No one can ever, ever take Joe's place but I know now that he would still want me to have a good life. You are a really, really special man. I'm sorry I've been wrapped up in my own sadness even though I knew you were also suffering." Jeannie reached across his body as they lay in bed and cuddled closer to him.

"It's so good to see my Jeannie back to the living world again," he said as he reached out and pulled her even closer. "Maybe we've both been going through the motions of living. Maybe there is magic in that red geranium. I didn't quite know what to think when I looked up and saw Bryan standing there trying to trade a potted plant for something to eat. And the rest just happened. It felt like the right thing to do. I guess I always knew I'd have your support. But you went off on your own when you opened the door of the hair salon. Do you think you'll be able to open it again?"

"Can I? I hope I can. I know it would be good for me to try to get back to what was our normal life. I can tell you miss it, Pete, and I hate being only part of the person

I used to be. My clients, the ones who used to be my most regular patrons, still call from time to time, to ask me to re-open the shop."

"Well, all any of us can do is try to make each day a good one."

"I have a question for you, Pete. Is the man named Einstein who told Bryan to trade the plant for food, the same man you brought home for dinner the night when we had the big storm about a year ago?"

"I guess so. He's driving a long distance rig now and back with his wife and children. He stops by the store every once in a while to say hello. I guess the good Lord must have put him on the road at exactly the right time and place so we could help Bryan."

"I think it was Bryan's grandmother who brought him here," Jeannie said as she drifted off to sleep.

The next morning after Pete had gone to work, Jeannie took the keys and went to the hair salon. After she unlocked the door she stood there a moment, gathering up her courage to try to see it in a new light. She sat in the chair remembering how she had set a playpen in the corner. Baby Joe would play there while she styled hair. She looked at the bulletin board behind the small reception desk where she posted a six-year old Joe's early attempts at art as well as the pictures drawn by the children of her clients. She remembered the fights she and Joe had when he was a teenager, especially when he wanted to take the car before he got his license. He was sure he would not get caught by the police and she was sure she wasn't going to give him the opportunity to test his theory. She seemed to hear his voice when he would rush into the salon announcing in a loud voice that he was dying of hunger. Throughout his short life he had wanted some very weird hair styles and color streaks in his hair that she hated. She was happy when he got through that stage of his life. As she thought about it, she realized that except for a couple of times while he was in college, she was the only person who had cut his hair until he went into the Army. She saw him everywhere she looked. She missed him so.

Jeannie thought back to the day she had opened her salon. Even as a small child she had been fascinated as she sat on the bed watching her mother at a dressing table brushing her own hair each night. Her mother would brush the long straight strands and pull them into a pony tail. In the morning she styled the hair into a bun or twist on the back of her head. Jeannie thought her mother was the most beautiful woman in the world. She wanted to learn how to style hair just like her mother. As a young child she styled her doll's hair and as a young woman she loved styling the hair of her friends. Her first job was in a local hair salon. Then she met Pete whose family owned the local store. She and Pete fell in love immediately and soon made wedding plans. Pete wanted Jeannie to have anything she wanted. Together they planned and built the home in which they now live. Jeannie was very, very happy but still was in love with hair styling. The small replica of the house was then built so Jeannie could have her own shop close to home. The shop was small but Jeannie's talent was large and her shop was very successful. When baby Joe was born, she felt like the luckiest and most loved person in the world. But that was before --- before Iraq and the loss of Joe.

As she sat reminiscing she took a good look at herself in the mirror. She was a middle-aged woman who looked old, tired and sad; not the enthusiastic-for-life woman she had been. Her skin had a sallow look. Her hair was shaggy and her body looked lumpy as she looked in the mirror. She looked like a very old woman. She seemed to live in her oldest clothes. She couldn't remember the last time she had gone shopping for anything new. The sweater she had on was at least ten years old. She realized she hadn't bought anything new to wear since Joe died. Her body showed the effects of all the time spent in a chair instead of moving around. She couldn't even remember the last time she had put on lipstick. Her hair was a mess. She hadn't had a professional haircut or even hair color since she closed the shop. She tried to cut her own hair and ended up with some bad results. Her sole employee, Gracie, had always cut and styled it for her. Jeannie realized she was stuck with an out-of-date look. She wondered if Gracie was still styling hair. Would Gracie come back to work for her if she re-opened her shop? Jeannie definitely would need someone to help her. She and Gracie had a system worked out so that one or the other was there each day. This left each of them with time for family events. But Jeannie had closed the shop with no thoughts of what the loss of a job would mean to Gracie. Or even to her regular customers. She owed both Gracie and her clients an apology.

Then she looked around the shop. It was a charming shop, but it definitely looked old. It certainly did not have a look of luxury, nor did it even seem pleasant to be in. There was no other word for it; it looked unloved and unoccupied.

She thought about her regular customers whom she had left without a hairdresser when she closed so quickly. As she sat there she realized she had not tried to keep her customers styled with the current fashions. She should have at least discussed up-to-date styles with them. She owed them something for her actions. But what could she do?

She thought about the two offers she had received to sell the shop, but she still saw Joe everywhere and would not even discuss the matter.

Jeannie thought about the money it would take to change things. Fortunately for her, the money needed to renovate was not a problem. Pete had insisted that the salon become a separate entity from their personal lives. She paid expenses and Gracie's salary out of that fund, but nothing for herself. She had a bank account that could fund some changes. But she had no idea how in the world to decide what things to change first. She needed help.

Her thoughts drifted to a childhood friend named Marcie who was also a born hair dresser. As children and young girls they were constantly styling not only each other's hair, but also that of their friends. Marcie now had two businesses in Pittsburgh: a beauty school and a large successful hair salon. Jeannie sat and thought for a while. Marcie is the person who could best help her decide what to do with the shop.

Since the phone service in the salon had been cancelled,

she returned to her house to call Marcie. But first, she needed to call Gracie. She could not imagine even opening the salon without Gracie's help.

"Gracie, how are you?" Jeannie asked.

"Jeannie? Well, how nice to hear from you. How have you been? I've really missed you."

"Gracie, I've been living in a tunnel with my eyes closed since Joe died. But my eyes are open now. I really just realized how stranded I left you when I closed the shop so suddenly. Please accept my apologies. I miss your friendship."

"Well, I certainly miss you. But I did understand. How are you? Are things okay for you now?"

"Within the last couple of weeks I have opened my eyes again. I want to move on with my life."

"What happened?"

"I was given a red geranium that I think is magical. It opened my eyes to the world around me. Actually that's why I calling. I'm thinking about opening the salon again. I know you are settled in a new place, but I trust you so much for good advice. Could we meet for lunch?"

"Just say where and what time. Let's do it tomorrow. I've really missed you, Jeannie."

Jeannie's next call was to her friend Marcie in Pittsburgh. They had a long talk about their childhood and young years, about the death of Joe, and Jeannie's closing of the shop. Marcie was excited to hear that the shop might re-open.

"What can I do to help?" she asked.

"I want an up-to-date shop with a little bit of luxury and I want to know how to cut the current hair styles."

"I'm just the person who can help you," Marcie said. "Why don't you come to Pittsburgh? I'll have one of our stylists show you some new methods. And we can check out some supply houses for any new equipment you might want."

"I may want to bring a friend. She worked for me for years but is at another salon now. I would really like her to see the new equipment and learn the new styles. I hope I can get her to come back here to work, but when I closed the shop so suddenly, she had to find a job in another salon. I treated her badly, but I'm hoping to make amends. Would you mind if I bring her?"

"Of course, bring her along."

Like a mother hen looks after her chicks, Jeannie continued to look after Bryan, insisting he had to have dinner with them at least one night a week and on the weekends. Bryan seemed happy to be with them, saying it gave his life a very nice routine and balance.

That night while the three of them were eating dinner Pete told Jeannie and Bryan about a call he had that day.

"It was Andy Fagan. Do you remember when he came to see me a couple of months ago?" he asked Jeannie. "He wants to stop by and see me this week."

"I think so. Isn't he the man from the big grocery chain who wants to buy the store?"

"Yes, he's the one."

"What? Sell the store?" Bryan asked. "You're the most

important man in town. You wouldn't really consider it would you?"

"Well, I told him I'd consider it. I had been wondering if it might be a good move for us to get away from here and get a new start somewhere else."

Jeannie spoke. "What Pete means is that he had been wondering if it would be good for me to move from the area. Pete's a good man and he loves me that much. But Pete, you don't need to do that for me. I know now that I'm going to be OK. I'm going to be busy running my business again. You can run your store with the same confidence you did before."

"Bryan, I hope someday you meet someone just as special as this woman. It makes life worthwhile."

"Were you ever married, Bryan?" Jeannie asked him. "A good-looking young man like you must have had many loves in his life."

"Just one. But when I started my downhill slide, I sent her away. She was too good to have to put up with me."

"Can you tell me about her?" she asked.

"We met on campus. The first time I saw her I fell in love with her. We had a lot of cheap dates: lectures at school, walking around campus and such. Her family welcomed me into their home. She came from a well-to-do family. They treated me as one of their own. They even came to Maine to meet my grandmother. But after my stays in various hospitals, I cut her out of my life. She deserved someone strong and loving; someone able to take care of her, not someone who could not live a normal life."

"Well, you reached the bottom of your down-hill slide.

You're on your way back up now. You'll either find her again or find someone new," Jeannie told him.

Pete sat there, ignoring their chatter, appearing lost in his thoughts. "I do have one idea I'm thinking of that might bring in a few new customers at the store, or at least make it a little more interesting for our regular customers. I'd like to have a Vendor Day once or twice a month. We could let the vendors set up tables to demonstrate their lines and maybe hand out free samples. We could cut up fresh fruit into small slices or cubes to sample. We could do the same thing with meats and cheeses."

"Salad dressings could be put in small sample cups for someone to test a veggie slice," Jeannie offered.

"Jeannie should work in the bakery baking chocolate chip cookies. I will never forget the smell of the chocolate the first morning I was here. I could have eaten a dozen of the cookies," Bryan suggested.

"That is a good idea," Pete said with some enthusiasm. "We could place the big floor fan right by the oven so everyone could smell it all over the store. I'm beginning to think it is a doable idea. In fact, maybe I'll move the fan into the bakery right away. Then the customers can smell the fresh bread we make each day. Maybe I'll call some vendors tomorrow to get some input. I think most of them will be interested in promoting their wares."

"Does this mean you will tell Andy you don't want to sell?" Jeannie asked him.

"I love this town and I love the store. We have a wonderful crew of people working there. What would happen to them if I sell the store? Most big chains have a certain set of standards that everyone must abide by. We seem to manage well working around school and family schedules. I doubt you could do that if you work for a big chain store."

"Well, Pete, I'll certainly support whatever decision you think best. You have always supported me through thick and thin, and it's been very thin lately," Jeannie said.

"Have you finally decided to reopen the shop?" Bryan asked her.

"I think I will," she answered. "Part of me wants to but what if I start to change things and then change my mind. What happens then?"

"Jeannie, what happens then is that you look for a support system. I really can understand your concerns. You and Pete are here for me. Now when I get that feeling I know I can come to you. Now, besides Pete, you have me in your life. I will do everything I can to help you. But I learned the hard way that sometimes you have to be willing to accept the help that someone wants to give you."

"Bryan, you're so encouraging to me. Maybe I should try it. But I've been thinking that I only want to do it if I can have the best shop in town. And to do that, I need to have more knowledge about the newest methods for cutting hair in a current style and the new equipment and supplies available. I don't want to do the set-hair styles that I did before."

"What's the best way to make that happen?" Pete asked.

"I think I'm going to go to Pittsburgh for a couple of days to see Marcie. She operates one of the top salons there. I called her and she said she'd help me get up-to-date on styles and equipment."

"Why don't you give her a call to tell her you'll be there?"

"I think I will." Jeannie got up and left the room. A few minutes later she was back with a big smile. "I'm going down there next week."

"Why don't you take Gracie with you? She'll need to know the latest procedures too. You'll need help if you ever want a day off," Pete said. Turning to Bryan he said, "Gracie was her assistant and best friend. We haven't seen much of her lately."

"I will do that," Jeannie said. "I did call Gracie today and apologized for the sudden closing of the salon. We're going to have lunch tomorrow. I'll ask her about going to Pittsburgh then."

Bryan spoke. "Maybe this is another door to open and claim your past life. You have been so encouraging to me; let me push you a little if you get discouraged."

Jeannie smiled and said, "Yes, boss."

Bryan stood up and reached for his coat. "Good. I've got to leave now. The morning comes very quickly when you sleep well at night."

Jeannie gave him a hug and then stepped back quickly to look at Bryan.

"Bryan, you've put on weight. I don't feel bones anymore. Just look at you," she said with a smile. "You need some new jeans. Your seams are almost splitting on those."

"Do you really think so?" Bryan said with a look of surprise. "If I do it's because of your good cooking."

"Look at your arms," Pete said. "I think it's from your workouts at the gym. You look terrific. I guess I haven't really looked at you for a while."

After Bryan left, Pete turned to Jeannie and said, "Don't you feel good that you were responsible for helping to change Bryan's life. I really think he's going to be OK."

"Well, I was terribly disappointed when he wanted to get his own place. I think I needed him as much as he needed us. But now I feel so proud of him." Then she added, "But there is one thing I will have to change. I had planned to give him Joe's clothes, a few pieces at a time. It's too late for that now. They would be too small."

As she busied herself in the kitchen that night her eyes fell on the red geranium. "I guess you are working your magic on me, too," she said aloud. "Save some magic for Pete. He tries to be strong for me but I know how he has grieved for his son."

While Jeannie was busy preparing for her upcoming trip to Pittsburgh, Pete was admitting that he could not sell the store. His grandparents had established one of the first gas stations in the area on the property where his supermarket was built. They sold only gasoline, candy, soda pop and chewing gum. Then his father, with the help of his mother, had expanded the retail section to sell bread, milk and a few other retail items.

When Pete had returned from Vietnam, he found his father and mother both had serious medical conditions and planned to close their little store. Pete knew he did not want that to happen. So he started to work hard, got a loan and took over the store. Little by little he expanded the items they carried until there was no room left in the building. He had a new building erected – the one now existing and the supermarket was in business. This store was like a child to him. He loved being there everyday. He loved the people who worked for him and looked to him for leadership. He loved seeing new products come in and non-selling items disappear. He loved this store. How could he consider selling it? It was a part of his life and legacy. At one time he had big dreams that the sign on the front would read Pete and Joe's or maybe Pete and Son. Even Joe had talked about that. Just before Joe shipped out for the last time, he reminded his dad to get the sign ready. How could he even think of selling the business? He knew he could never do that.

When he had lunch with Andy later that week, he told him he had decided not to sell. He loved this town, he loved the people and he loved his store.

The store was well run. There was no reason he had to be there every day. Maybe, Pete mused, he and Jeannie could go on a cruise in January before she opens her shop again. Jon Webster had proven many times he was a competent manager at the grocery store. Their staff was well-trained. They were all very loyal to the store and each other. He wondered what the employees there would think about his idea for a Vendor Day. The staff all knew that he had been approached about selling the store. He decided it was time to share his decision not to sell the store and share his ideas for improving sales with his staff. After all, they were like family. They supported him so much in the days when they learned of Joe's death. Pete wanted them to be a part of his planning. He decided to ask the staff to come to work a half-hour early the next morning, and also ask the late staff to come in for a special meeting at 7 a.m. Then he went to talk with Jon to tell him of his plans.

The next morning Pete could see some concern on the faces of his staff as he met with them. He made a big urn of coffee and set out fresh pastries as they gathered in the small lunch room area of the store. After greeting them and thanking them for their past support he began to talk.

"Most of you already know I was approached with an offer to buy the store. I have made a decision that I will not sell the store." A small cheer went up from the staff. "But I do have some ideas I want to share with you. I would like you to listen and think about them and think of your own ideas on how we can change this store to make it a nicer place for our customers to shop."

His idea to have a Vendor Day was met with enthusiasm. Other ideas were suggested to help the traffic flow a little easier and one employee suggested they resurface the parking lot and offer wider spaces to park. It was a very meaningful session. Everyone was enthusiastic about upcoming changes.

"There is one last thing I would like to say in closing. I am pleased to announce that Jon Webster is being promoted to Store Superintendent effective immediately. I may not always be at the store each day, but I know that the store will be well managed by Jon and each of you."

The promotion idea had come to Pete as he drove to work. He knew it was the right thing to do. Jon had been there for him through all the days of his troubles and kept things running smoothly. Jon needed to be recognized for his efforts.

The following week Pete approached Bryan one day at the store.

"Got plans for tonight?" he asked Bryan.

"Probably just work out at the gym," Bryan answered.

"Jeannie's in Pittsburgh for a couple of days. Let's go to the steak house for dinner. Got a couple of ideas I'd like to talk over with you."

"That sounds great. I got something I want to talk over with you, too."

The two men made small talk while they ate their dinner. As they had some coffee Pete said, "I have a big favor to ask of you, Bryan. But if you feel it would put too much pressure on you, please be honest with me. What I'm going to ask doesn't have to be done in one day."

"What's on your mind?" Bryan asked.

"For the first time since Joe died, Jeannie and I are doing OK, so I want to be careful about our next steps. As you know, Jeannie will be re-opening her shop. We are going to remodel it. We are tentatively planning for the renovation of her shop to start right after the holidays. That's where my problem comes in. For some time before you showed up on our doorstep I was desperate to try to help Jeannie. I felt I needed to take her away for a while. I made tentative plans for Jeannie and me to go on a southern Atlantic cruise in January. We will leave from Florida, go through the Panama Canal and then head for California. She knows nothing about this; I want it to be a Christmas present. With all the changes to her shop beginning in January, someone needs to be at the house to oversee things.

"But that's not all. With the changes we are making at the store, I am worried about putting too much pressure on Jon. He's really smart and capable but there is no good back up for him to deal with problems. Would it put too much pressure on you to oversee both projects so I can take Jeannie away? If you want time to think about it, take a couple of days. You have made a miraculous recovery since you have been here. It would not be fair to put any pressure on you if you are not yet ready for it."

"Pete, you and Jeannie have made me feel like I could take on the world's problems and solve them. I think you have a wonderful idea. You should forget the store for a couple of weeks. Jon is so smart and I'll be beside him to boost his morale if need be. And if I see anything going wrong at the salon, I'll just call you. I think it will be a wonderful time for you."

"There is something else going on," Pete said quietly. "Our mayor has privately told a few of us that he must resign due to medical reasons. I have been asked to serve as the temporary mayor until a new election is held next fall. I first said no, but I'm being pressured to consider it. I have a couple of weeks to decide."

"Pete, that's wonderful. This town could not get anyone more qualified to be mayor. You already take care of everyone in town. You would be the best mayor ever. What did Jeannie say about it?"

"I haven't told her yet. She's so excited about re-opening her shop I thought I'd wait a while to tell her."

"She'll be very happy for you."

"Well, you can see I have a lot on my mind. But I want to know about you. Bryan, be honest with me. How do you really feel about the way your life is going these days?"

"Pete, you and Jeannie have given me a family and a home, regardless of where I hang my hat. I feel like I have the tigers of the past by the tail. I sleep well at night and I'm healthier than I have been for years."

"You are qualified to do so many things. I know we can't expect you to water plants in the grocery store for much longer. I know you said you wanted six months to prove yourself but do you think about your future?"

"Yes, I guess I do. Meyer Higgs took me for coffee last week." Pete knew that Meyer Higgs owned the floral business that rented space in Pete's store.

"Did he say anything interesting?" Pete asked.

"He has been pleased with the increase in sales of the flowers and plants at the store. He is getting ready to retire and asked me if I would like to buy his business. I told him a little about my past and how you befriended me. I told him I felt I needed six months with no relapse before I make any decisions about my future. Then he offered me a job to manage his business for the next few months with the idea that I would have first chance to buy his business at that time. He said he would be willing to wait for me. He said he would do this because he thinks I can make a success of what has become a failing business. I told him

I would think about it and try to give him an answer after the first of the year."

"That's wonderful, Bryan. I'm sure you could make a success of it. You certainly have made a success of the department at our store. I really believe you could do it."

"Pete, think about all the pros and cons about me doing it. You probably know me better than anyone on earth. After you come back from your cruise, I'll come to you for your official opinion. I don't want to rush into anything. I want to make the right decision."

The men sat quietly pondering the changes that were taking place in their lives.

"Bryan, do you think we both are feeling the magic of a certain plant?" Pete asked

"I don't know, Pete, but it does give me an idea. If I ever open my own flower shop or greenhouse, I think I'll name it, The Red Geranium."

Jeannie and Pete stopped living by rote. No longer did they get out of bed to greet the day with the same routine. Now they got up, hurried through breakfast, shared their busy plans for the day and went his or her own way.

But every day, they each found time to stop and smile at the red geranium.

Chapter 4
Alma

Alma was the stereotype of the little old woman who lived alone atop a mountain. She was small in size and had thin white wiry hair that probably hadn't been cut in years. She had two or maybe three loose fitting dresses that she had owned for many years but she preferred a pair of over-sized work pants and work shirts that had been her husband's. She was a proud woman who asked for nothing.

Her home was located up a very steep driveway near the top of one of the Allegheny Mountains. The view from the windows that circled under the eaves of the house afforded her a spectacular view. You could see for miles an ever-changing scene: snow covered woods in the winter, the pale green of the leaves along with the flowering blossoms in the spring, the lush fullness of many different trees with leaves of many shades of red and green in the summer, and the beauty of the reds, yellows, and rust colored leaves in the fall.

About once or twice a week she would walk down the mountain trail into town to Pete's Groceries to pick up a few cans of something or maybe a loaf of bread. On her way back she would stop at her mailbox. She used to get a Social Security check once a month but they had stopped coming. It was a good thing she had some money stashed in a shoe box to pay for her food. Her Henry had been a good man to provide for her needs. He had told her he had arranged for her to get a check each month for the rest of her life. Now times had changed. But she wasn't worried. If she was careful with the money in the shoebox, she should be okay for a couple of more years. One problem was that the walk down to Pete's seemed to be getting longer and harder. Pete had business interests down the road beyond her house. Almost always he would drive her home on his way to do errands or have someone else do them so they could drop her off at home. She was grateful for the ride. And while she might have been able to buy more groceries at one time, since she might get a ride home, her trip to the store was the only contact she had with the outside world. She had no close neighbors to talk with.

On a cold wet day like today she had been very happy when Pete had asked the young man named Bryan to drive her home. She thought Bryan was a nice enough young man but something about him disturbed her a little. She had a feeling that he might not be able to see how happy she was living alone without the bother of company around. Oh, well, he did bring her home. She went out to a shed, chopped some of the firewood she had brought from the woods, and then opened a can of soup and had her evening meal. As the dark shadows of night fell around the house, she climbed into bed with a well-worn book and her flashlight and settled in for the night.

The next day Alma got up early, bundled up in her heavy clothes and went to the woods. She was getting low on firewood so she gathered up armloads of branches and decayed lumber and carried it to the shed. She knew the snows would soon start to fall and it might get difficult for her to leave the house. Two things Henry had done were helping her now. When the house was built, it had taken some months for the gas and electric companies to run lines this far up the mountain, so she and Henry had put an old wood-burning cook stove in a sort of shelter which they could use while the house was being completed. As the house was built he also had put in a big fireplace along a wall in the living room so they could keep warm. When the house was finished, he closed in and kept the kitchen with the wood-burning stove on the new house. Now the old stove came in handy for cooking and heat on the cool mornings. For many years she had used it when she did her canning in the summertime because of the nice breeze that blew through the area. Now that it was winter she had a way to keep warm and heat her food that cost her no money. She didn't understand why her electric and gas didn't work any more but she could manage without them. Today she found some pieces of cardboard in one of the sheds and carried them to the house to dry out. There was a draft coming in around one of her windows and she wanted to be ready for the mountain's cold winter winds.

Alma hadn't always lived this way. When she and Henry had built this house she felt like she was a millionaire. Henry had situated the house on the lot and placed windows under the eaves so that from every window she could see for miles across the valleys below. The home was nicely furnished and they loved to entertain. Many times hikers or cross-country skiers would come by. In the winter she would invite them in and make hot coffee or tea and let them rest a while in front of the big fireplace before moving on. In the summertime she served lemonade or iced tea on the big veranda that surrounded the house. They had a good life that was made even better when their daughter, Mindy, was born. Henry had insisted that Mindy go to the finest boarding schools and university. Mindy found a new way of life in the city and urged her parents to move to be close to her and just vacation at the mountain retreat, but Alma and Henry had declined. When Mindy had tried to insist, harsh words had been said and Henry had told Mindy to leave and to never come back again. She did come back when Henry died and urged Alma to move into town. But Alma was becoming more and more of a loner. She needed no one to help her. She wanted to prove that she was a strong and independent woman.

A few days after returning home with Bryan, it was time to go back down the mountain to go to the store. She needed to get some coffee and maybe she'd even buy a couple oranges. Somehow that sounded very good to her.

The young man named Bryan welcomed her.

"Well, hello, Alma. You must have had a cold slippery walk today."

"The walk keeps me young, I think," Alma told him.

"That must be so because you're looking very chipper," he told her. "Let me know when you're ready to leave and I'll drop you off at home. Pete's got an errand to be made out your way."

"Thank you kindly. That would be very nice." Alma had to bite her cheeks a bit as she said the words but she knew the ride home would be helpful. Maybe she would buy an extra can of soup or maybe even more oranges since she wouldn't have to carry them home. She might get snowed in one of these days.

After she had put a few things in her basket she went to look for Bryan. She found him in the section where they sold fresh flowers and plants. The area looked like summer with buckets filled with blooming flowers. For a moment Alma just stood and looked around amazed to see such beauty when just beyond the windows she could see snow start to fall.

"Are you ready to leave now?" Bryan asked her. "I'll meet you at the door. Just let me tell Pete I'm leaving."

Alma waited at the door. She saw Pete and Bryan approach her. Bryan was carrying a bouquet of fresh cut flowers with a beautiful pink rosebud in the center.

"That's the most beautiful bouquet I've ever seen," Alma told him.

"This is for you. Some of the flowers are a few days old. You might as well enjoy them," Bryan said.

Pete spoke up and said, "Alma, Thanksgiving is

coming this week. Jeannie, Bryan and I will be celebrating together. We would like you to join us. Bryan will pick you up around one and take you home after dinner."

"I don't think I'll be able to make it," Alma told him.

"Then I won't have a date for dinner," Bryan told her. "Please come long enough for one of Jeannie's good dinners, then I'll drive you home. I'll have my new car by then. Well, it's a used car but it's new to me. I need to see if it's got enough pep to get up your mountain."

Alma didn't quite know what to say. The walk up the mountain was a bit tough for her and if she told him no, well, he might not drive her home. And to have something cooked that was not from a can did sound good.

When Bryan took her home he told her he would pick her up on Thursday at one o'clock.

Alma didn't know what to do on Thanksgiving morning. She definitely did not want to go to Pete's house for dinner. She was happier spending her days alone. But if she offended Pete by not going, he might stop driving her home from the store. That walk up the mountain was hard. Anyhow, her phone didn't work any more and she had no way to contact Bryan to tell him not to come for her. She finally decided she had to go.

She pulled out one of her dresses. It must have been years since she had it on and it was very big on her small frame. *I guess Henry liked me fat and sassy,* she thought. She tried to smooth her hair back but it wouldn't stay in place. She finally found a rubber band and pulled it back into a bun. She found her old coat that she had thought about taking apart to make into a blanket. The wool in the coat would make the blanket hold lots of warmth. But it was still a coat today so she put it on and went to the window to watch for Bryan's car. When she saw the car pull into the yard she hurried out so he wouldn't come into the house.

"Alma, you look very nice. I hope you brought a good appetite with you. Jeannie is a wonderful cook."

"It's been a while since I shopped for clothes."

"Well, you look very nice and appropriate for the occasion. I bet Jeannie has a feast prepared for us."

Alma sat quietly without speaking during the drive down the mountain.

Jeannie and Pete were at the door to welcome them. "We're so glad you came today. Thanksgiving is about being with family. Now that there are four of us, we are a family celebrating together," Jeannie said as she welcomed her.

They stepped into the dining room. Alma saw a big table set with a beautiful linen cloth and fine china plates and sterling silverware. There were candles burning in tall holders. For a moment Alma remembered all the Thanksgiving dinners she had prepared. She and Henry always invited their friends to share Thanksgiving dinner. Then Henry had died and her cooking days ended. For a moment she thought she might cry. She swallowed hard. "Can I help with anything?" she offered.

"I'd appreciate that. Would you prepare a couple of relish trays for us? I've got jars of pickles and olives ready for one tray and raw vegetables for the other."

Alma was glad to be busy. She went to the kitchen. On the kitchen table sat a tall bright red geranium. Alma felt drawn to go and touch the plant. "It's a red geranium," she said softly. "I haven't seen one for years."

"Isn't it beautiful?" Jeannie asked. She stopped her work and came to the table. "It's a magic geranium. Don't laugh at me when I say that because I really think it is magic. Bryan showed up at the store one day carrying this plant. It seems he'd been living a very hard life and someone gave it to him. It brought back lots of good memories for him and he decided to change his life. And I think you will agree he's a wonderful young man. Anyhow, he gave it to Pete in exchange for a sandwich and Pete brought it home and gave it to me." Jeannie put down the bowl she had in her hands and touched the plant. "Just like it inspired Bryan to change his life, somehow or other it changed my life also. I know I was in a state of denial and grief ever since we heard of Joe's death. But this plant has brought me hope. Now I've got my life back on track again. I'm going to reopen my hair salon and I've started to see people and live again. I truly think the plant is magical."

Alma spoke. "It reminds me of my honeymoon. Henry and I went to Europe. When we were in Austria every house had window boxes filled with red geraniums. All over town we saw them. We decided our mountain home would have window boxes with red geraniums every summer. After Henry got sick we stopped planting them. I had forgotten all about them." Alma stood there quietly with her hand on the plant, lost in her thoughts.

"Time to eat," Pete announced, so they gathered around the table. Alma was surprised at how much she ate, but also how much she talked. It was the first meal she had eaten with another person in maybe two or three years.

As Alma and Jeannie cleared the table after dinner, Jeannie placed a stack of small containers on the table. "I want you and Bryan both to take home some of everything on the table. Then we can remember the good time we've had here today sharing this meal." Jeannie got two shopping bags and put the food containers inside.

Alma stood looking out the kitchen windows. "That's a pretty little house next door. Who lives there? Is it family?"

"No, that's my hair salon. When we heard our Joe had been killed in Iraq, I shut the door and said I'd never open it again. But maybe it was the magic of the red geranium. I am re-opening it. Many of my old regular customers have said they will return. I will always miss Joe for he was full of life and spirit. I know he'd be happy to see me return to live a normal life." She stood there quietly deep in thought. "Maybe you'd like to see inside the little house. I have keys right here."

"Maybe some other time," Alma said. "I should be getting back up the mountain. I'm afraid we're in for a storm. The sky is so dark. The roads may turn slick with this snow falling."

"I'll take you when you're ready," Bryan said.

As they went to leave the house, Jeannie took the red geranium from the table. "I know I'm going to be okay now. Maybe this geranium will bring you happy thoughts," she said as she placed the plant in Alma's arms.

Alma was so excited to be given the plant she thought

she would cry, but she went through the motions of saying she shouldn't take it. Jeannie insisted, so Alma and Bryan left the house with two bags of food and a red geranium.

There was snow falling and the roads were becoming slick as she and Bryan drove back up the mountain. When they reached her house everything seemed dark and still. He pulled up the driveway that ended at her back door.

"I see two lamp posts out front but no lights came on. Don't you need the outside lights to come on when you return home?" Bryan asked her. "Here, let me carry the bag and plant for you."

"My outside lights don't work any more," she told him. "You don't have to walk me to the door. I've got everything."

"Nonsense," Bryan said. "I'll see you safely inside. I wouldn't sleep tonight if I didn't know you were safe. Why don't I come back in the morning and see if I can fix your lights?"

"No, no, that isn't necessary," Alma said, almost shoving him out the door.

She quickly said good night and closed the door.

Alma went inside, sat down and cried. *How did my life spin so out of control? Henry, I need you*, she thought. She sat on a kitchen chair, holding the red geranium close to her body.

Bryan was puzzled by the abrupt send off from Alma. He didn't even see her turn a light on in the house. As he made his way down the mountain he felt very puzzled. Well, there was just one answer for him. He'd see if Pete would give him the next day off. He'd take the tools he was accumulating and go back to Alma's in the morning. Maybe he could do some small repairs for her to get her outside lights working. It may be that all the lights needed were new light bulbs.

Alma sat holding the red geranium for some time and then got her flashlight and book and went to bed. The room seemed cold and empty after having shared the fellowship of Bryan, Pete and Jeannie. She placed the red geranium close to her bed. At times she thought maybe it wasn't real and if she closed her eyes it would disappear.

She was happy when she saw the geranium still by her bed in the morning. She carried it with her when she went to start fires in the fireplace and cook stove. She heard a car coming up the driveway. "Who could that be?" she asked herself as she went to the window. She looked out and saw Bryan getting out of his car. He reached inside the car and removed a tool box and a bag as he made his way to her front door.

Alma didn't know what to do. No one had been in her house for years. She wasn't prepared for company. She had a thought that she might pretend she wasn't home and maybe he'd go away, but remembering how he had insisted on walking her to the door last night, it made her think that he'd probably just wait for her to come back home, or maybe even break a window to make sure she was okay.

Bryan seemed to pause for a couple of minutes and she could hear him walking to the left and right of the front door. Finally, she heard him knock and call out to her.

"Alma, it's Bryan. Please let me in. I brought us some fresh donuts and hot coffee."

As she slowly opened the door he gently pushed by her and stepped into the house. "Good morning, did you sleep well last night?" he asked.

"I'm not ready to receive company," she told him. She suddenly became aware that both the kitchen and dining room tables were stacked high with papers, magazines, mugs half filled with cold coffee and dirty dishes. The inside of the room was filled with clutter. There had been nothing swept or dusted for months. She had no place for them to sit to have coffee.

"Let's take the coffee and donuts and sit on the sofa and talk," Bryan said.

"Why did you come here today? I told you I was O.K."

"Because I want to be your friend. I thought maybe the bulbs had burned out in your outdoor lights and I could replace them for you. But now I don't think burned out light bulbs are the problem. Tell me, Alma, do you use your front door very often?"

"No, I always use the back door. It's closer to the driveway."

"Well, that may explain something." Bryant paused,

and then gently said, "Alma, do you have someone you call on to help you with your business and financial matters?"

"No, I'm an independent woman. I can do it myself," she said crossly.

Bryan paused for a moment and then quietly began to talk. "Alma, I'm not sure how to say this but I like you too much to let this go on. Forgive me if I seem too nosy. But Alma, there were notices on your front door that have apparently been there for a long time."

"What kind of notices?"

"These kinds." Bryan laid out notices from the utility and phone companies that they were shutting off service. "Apparently your payments didn't reach them. Do you remember making payments to them?" Bryan paused and then continued. "And this red paper is a notice that the state is foreclosing on your property because you have paid no taxes on it for some time."

Alma started to sob quietly. Bryan went to sit next to her and put his arms around her. They sat quietly for a few minutes. Then Bryan spoke softly.

"I know you are a proud independent woman. I'll help you take care of this matter if you'll let me."

With a sob in her voice Alma began to talk. "It all started when the government stopped sending me a Social Security check. I used to get a check. I'd take it into the bank and cash it and pay my bills. But one day the checks stopped coming. Henry always kept a supply of cash in a shoe box for emergencies. I found I could get by without electricity by using flashlights. I needed no phone, and the fireplace keeps me warm. I have the woods to supply me with firewood and so I keep the cash to buy food."

"The companies were required by law to send you an official notice of shut-off. Do you remember getting any?"

"No, but I have a lot of mail on the table I didn't open. At first I kept thinking I'd get another Social Security check and everything would be OK. I guess I just forgot about paying bills after a time." Alma sat quietly, bent over slightly with her head in her hands. "I don't know what to do now. I don't know where I'll go to live if they take my house."

"How about your daughter? Don't you think she'd want to know about all this?"

"She'll think I'm old and stupid. Well, maybe I am."

"Alma, you are not old and stupid. Everyone needs help from time to time. I certainly did. Pete and Jeannie were there for me. Now, let me help you. Or we can call Pete. He knows everyone in town and could probably straighten things out quickly."

"I'm embarrassed by this mess. Does everyone have to know about it?"

"I'm sure Pete will be very discrete. Can I call and ask him to come up here?"

There were a couple minutes of silence. Then Alma spoke. "I don't know what to do."

"Then let me make the decision for you. Let me call Pete. I'll put the call on speaker. You listen to what I say and if you want me to stop talking, I will."

Bryan reached for his cell phone and dialed Pete's number.

"Hi Bryan, did you run into some problem and need a different tool?" Pete asked in a cheerful voice.

"Pete, I'm with Alma now and we have you on the speaker phone. I have located the problem but it is a different problem than I thought. It is a serious problem and we need your help. Do you think you could come up here any time soon?"

"Henry and Alma were good citizens of our town. If I can help any way, I certainly will. I'll be there in half an hour. Do I need to bring tools or anything?"

"Just your kind heart, Pete. We'll see you soon."

Bryan asked Alma if she was O.K.

"Just embarrassed and sad, I guess," Alma said.

"Let's start going through the mail on the table. Let's get it sorted out so we can see if we are missing anything important."

Bryan brought a large arm load of mail from the dining room table, placed it on the floor, and started to sort it: all the monthly utility bills in one pile etc. and junk mail in another. Bryan noticed what appeared to be statements from the bank. He placed them in another pile. There was mail from the state, probably advising her about her failure to pay the taxes.

"I didn't realize how much I have accumulated and forgetful I have been. Do you think I'll lose my house? I don't know what to do." She sat quietly on the floor, surrounded by mail, and again began to weep very quietly.

Bryan put down the mail in his hand and sat on the floor beside her. He put his arms around her and let her cry.

Pete was there in less then twenty minutes. He came to the front door, knocked and then opened the door.

"You two have me curious about what's going on," he began and then paused as he saw Alma and Bryan sitting on the floor surrounded by mountains of mail.

"You tell him, Bryan. I'm too ashamed."

"Alma, don't ever be ashamed in front of me," Pete said. "Start at the beginning and tell me everything."

"I'm losing my house because I didn't pay the taxes. And I didn't pay any of my bills so I have no gas, electric, or telephone. I forgot all about paying bills. At first I thought I'd pay them when I got my Social Security check but I don't get a check any more."

"What do you mean, you don't get a Social Security check?"

"I don't get a check any more. They stopped sending them."

"Did you ask anyone why they stopped?"

"No. I just figured I'd used up all the money Henry had paid in."

"Does Mindy know about all this?"

"No, and please don't tell her. She'll send me off to some poorhouse to end up my days."

"Mindy is your daughter. She has a right to know."

"Please, please don't tell her."

"I'll make you no promises. Let's see if we can straighten it out."

Bryan had returned to sorting the mail. "I think I may have a clue. Alma, may I open this bank statement and look at it?"

"I don't care," she told him.

Bryan opened the envelope and began to smile. "It is just what I thought it might be." He began to laugh out loud as he placed the bank statements into her hands. "Look at the bottom figure. You are a rich lady, Alma."

"I don't understand," she said as she looked at the amount. She handed the statement to Pete.

"I think I know what happened," Bryan said. "The Social Security office stopped sending paper checks to most people. They simply transfer the amount to your bank account. You must have furnished them with the account number at one time. Each month the amount of your check is deposited into your account. You have withdrawn no funds from the account. Alma, you have plenty of money to live whatever life style you choose."

"I still don't understand," Alma said.

Slowly and gently, Pete and Bryan again explained how automatic deposits worked.

"How do I get out of this mess?" she asked.

"We start by paying your back taxes and utility bills. Then you must decide if you want to stay by yourself on top of the mountain or join the rest of the world." Pete spoke quietly and calmly. "Please do this for me. Let me talk to Mindy. Mindy calls me from time to time to check on you. I had no idea you were living without modern conveniences. I should have been more alert. You need to think about your future. Do you want to continue to live up here the way you have been living, without friends or anyone to help you? Or would you like to join the world of the living and maybe come up here for vacations? You are a bright, intelligent woman, Alma. Henry was very proud of you."

"He'd be disappointed if he saw me now," Alma said.

"Then why not change the way you live now. We'll help you," Bryan said.

"Does Mindy have to know how bad all this mess is?" she asked again.

They all sat quietly for a few minutes.

Then Pete spoke "Maybe not. If you're serious about changing your life, Bryan and I will help you get this mess straightened out. We can get it started this morning. But then you must call Mindy. You can tell her as much or as little as you please. But you must stay in touch with her. Can you live with those conditions?"

Alma sat quietly, saying nothing.

Bryan spoke. "Alma, for a long time I thought I needed no one. I ended up sleeping on a piece of cardboard along a busy highway. My mind was very confused. I thought of nothing except how to get through the next hour. But one night someone left that red geranium by my side. I walked away that night, carrying the plant. With Pete's and Jeannie's help, I joined the world of the living. It's a wonderful world. But no one can make you ready for the world. It will be up to you. I know you can do it because I did. And I'll help you all I can while you make changes. But bottom line, it will be up to you to be willing to change."

"I'm scared," Alma said.

"We'll be here for you," Pete said. Then with a smile he added, "We need a woman's view on things. Let's get

Jeannie up here. She can help you get some new clothes so you can become the woman you used to be."

"Would she help me with my hair?"

"I'm sure she would if you ask her. Bryan, call Jeannie and tell her I'm here and we need her woman's touch to help Alma. I'm going to call George Henderson at the bank. I think he can help us make short work of all this business."

George Henderson was the president at the local bank. George said he would personally call the utility and county offices to get the necessary amounts and transfer the funds to get the procedure started to restore power to her home. He would also see that the taxes were paid.

Jeannie arrived quickly. After being briefed about the situation, she soon had Pete and Bryan busy starting to clear out the clutter and clean the floors and windows. Jeannie checked Alma's clothes and found very little worth saving. She took Alma to her home where she fixed a perfumed bath for Alma to soak in while she brought her tea and snacks. Then she cut and styled Alma's hair. This was followed by a shopping trip for clothes and a few new things for her home.

When they arrived home very late that afternoon, two rooms had been cleaned and there were groceries in the cabinets.

Alma was full of smiles and laughter when she and Jeannie returned to the house.

The men made a big fuss over the transformation of her new appearance and clothes and the women made a big fuss over the transformation of Alma's house. "It's magical," one of them said.

"Like the magic of the red geranium?" Alma asked.

Pete and Bryan looked at each other. "Who knows?" Pete said. "Maybe that plant is magical."

That night as Alma put on a new nightgown and got into the bed with new sheets and blankets she felt like a queen. She knew now the house she and Henry had shared was hers forever. The back taxes had been paid. And within the next two days her utility services would be working. She would have heat from the furnace again and electric lights and a telephone. She got out of bed and went to the bathroom to take another look in the mirror. She couldn't quite believe the change in her appearance. *I look so good* she thought with a smile on her face. While Bryan and Pete had taken care of her business and house matters, Jeannie had worked her magic on Alma. The long, wiry hair was now cut into a short bob which had soft, natural curls. While shopping, Alma got two new dresses, new slacks and tops, a new coat and jacket along with new shoes and personal items. Alma had been so excited that she insisted on throwing away the clothes she had been wearing. Along the way they had stopped for a fancy lunch and then went for high tea in the afternoon. Alma couldn't remember the last time she had eaten so much. Now as she lay in bed she was sure she was too excited to ever sleep again. But then she thought of something so got out of bed once more. She went to the kitchen to retrieve the red geranium and brought it to her bedside.

"Nobody had better tell me that this plant is not magic" she exclaimed.

About a week later, Alma surveyed her home while wearing her new brown slacks and a matching top that was so soft it felt like a blanket on her shoulders.

Bryan, Pete, and Jeannie had worked hard to get rid of the clutter in her home and now it not only looked terrific but it smelled fresh, too. The house was nice and warm from the gas furnace and the electric lamps made a soft glow in the room. She could look out clean windows and enjoy the view of the snow falling around her. Now she could see herself in the mirror in the dining room. "I look good," she again told herself.

But she realized that there was one thing more for her to do. She needed to call Mindy. She started to recall how set in his ways Henry got as he got older. Apparently, just the way she got set in her ways recently. *We wanted Mindy to become a strong independent woman, yet as soon as she did so, Henry put her out. Were we really being fair to her?* Alma sat and thought about the situation and what possible outcomes could be. She knew Mindy could not move her family here to the mountain. It would not be the right thing to do. Alma also knew that she should not expect strangers to try to come up the mountain to provide help for her. She, Alma, needed to move to the city, not to live with Mindy, but maybe somewhere close enough that she could call on her for help. *Maybe I do need to sell this wonderful home, or maybe I can find a way to live in the city in the winter and spend my summers here.*

Alma reached for her phone to call Mindy.

"Hello?"

Alma heard her daughter's voice for the first time in a long while.

"Mindy, it's Mom. How are you?"

"Mom… oh Mom… I'm so glad to hear your voice. Are you OK? I haven't been able to reach you by phone for some time now. Are you O.K?" she asked again.

"Mindy, I'm doing very well for someone my age. But I am lonesome to see you. Is there any chance you could possibly come to see me? You know I sold your Dad's car some time ago so I can't come to see you."

"Absolutely," Mindy said. "Today is Friday. Is tomorrow too soon to come up?"

"That would be wonderful. I think the time has come for me to move a little closer to civilization. I would like to have your opinion and suggestion on how to make that happen."

"Mom, Tom has to be back on Sunday but if it's OK with you, we will leave here early in the morning and be at your place before lunch. We'll have all afternoon to visit." Mindy paused and then went on. "Mom, I've been so worried about you. I just want to see you and hold your hand."

As Alma hung up the phone she felt relieved that she had taken the first step to bring about a reconciliation with her daughter; yet she felt nervous about how much to tell Mindy about what had happened. She reached for her phone and called Pete.

"Well, I did it. I called Mindy," she told him when he answered his phone.

"What was her reaction? Was she angry with you?"

"No, I believe she was really happy to hear from me. She and Tom are coming here tomorrow just for the day. Pete, I do think maybe it is time for me to move closer to Mindy or at least closer to help. Do you think I should tell her about the Social Security checks?"

"Alma, only you can make that decision. I will say nothing to her about it if I see her."

"Well, I'll sleep on it tonight. I owe you, Jeannie and Bryan a million dollars for helping me get back my life. Thank you so much."

Alma didn't sleep too well that night. She practiced over and over again the things she thought she would, or maybe would not, tell Mindy. She got up early the next morning, dusted the furniture and ran the sweeper. She wanted Mindy to see a clean house.

A little after ten o'clock she heard a car pull into her driveway. Alma was so nervous she was afraid she would fall over. She need not have worried. Mindy embraced her mother tightly and would not let her go. Finally, Tom, Mindy's husband, with a happy smile moved the women from the doorway. He was followed by a young man.

"I was afraid I might never see you again," Mindy began.

"Mindy, it was very wrong for me to treat you as I did. Can you forgive me?"

"Oh, Mom, of course, I can. Can you forgive me for not making you a part of our family life?"

"Maybe we both needed time apart," Alma said as she reached out to greet Tom and her grandson.

"This is Zack, our youngest son," Mindy told her.

"What a handsome young man you are," she told him. "You were just a baby the last time I saw you, but look at you now."

"Alma, it's been way too long since we've been together," Tom said as he gave her a hug. "You made your daughter really, really happy when you called her."

"Let's go to the kitchen and have coffee," Alma suggested. "You must be tired after your long trip."

Mindy stood looking out the windows. "I had forgotten how really beautiful it is up here," she said.

"Is there skiing near here?" Zack asked.

"Yes. There are many trails for skiing and ponds and outside skating rinks in the area. Within five miles there are various ski slopes, but cross-country skiing and snow shoeing are very popular too."

"Can we check it out, Dad?"

"I think that's a good idea. Let me show you around the area while your Mom and Grandma talk. We'll be back in plenty of time to take everyone out for lunch so don't try to fix anything."

"Mom, can I ask Grandma about..." Zack began.

"Ask me what, Zack?" Alma said.

Mindy spoke "I have told the kids about the evenings of music we used to have here. Zack and his friends have a band. He would love to see Dad's old guitar if you still have it."

"Of course I still have it. I'll get it out so you can take it home with you if you want it," Alma said.

"Let's do that later," Tom said. "Come on, Zack. Let's let these women talk. We'll see you later."

As soon as the men had gone, Mindy and Alma made their way to the sofa in the living room.

"Mom, you look positively radiant. I expected to see you all worn out and a house filled with clutter. But you look so beautiful and up to date. You look like you're my sister. And the house is sparkling. What is going on?"

Alma hesitated for a moment and then decided it was time for the truth. She told Mindy about how she had been living and how much help she had from Pete, Jeannie, and Bryan to start a new life.

"I know I could get stranded up here in the snow and maybe need help to get supplies. But I don't know if it is time to sell the house just yet. Most of all I don't want you or anyone else worrying about me. I know I need to change things but I don't know what to do. Will you help me?"

"Of course I will. I would love to have you living either with me or near me. There are so many options available. There are retirement villages where you could have your own apartment or condo and do all your own cooking. There are units where you live alone but take your meals with others. Another choice might be a residential room. You would have your own room in a big house with three other women. You would all take your meals together and socialize together when you want company. There is one close to us owned and run by two sisters who were nurses. One still works part-time. Or you could move in with Tom and me. Our two oldest kids are away at school and Zack will be going to college next fall. Tom has always said you are welcome to come and live with us."

"Oh my, I didn't know about all that. I thought I'd have to live in some poor house, probably living in a dormitory. Would I need to decide right away?" Alma asked.

"You don't have to decide right now. Why not plan to come to our house for Christmas? We'll take you around to see what's available and you can make up your mind after you see them all."

"Maybe I could get Bryan to bring me down."

"Tom and Zack have already said they'd come back next week to bring you home. Can I tell them you'll come?"

Alma paused for a moment. She wanted time to think things over, but she remembered how she had drifted for so many years and how good it felt to have her life back to normal.

"Yes," she said. "I'll come."

She heard the men coming in the door. "Anyone hungry for lunch?" she heard Tom ask.

"Give me ten minutes," Alma said. "Zack, will you come with me?" She took him to one of the bedrooms that had been closed off for years. "Get ready to sneeze from the dust," she told him.

They entered the room and Alma went to the corner and removed the guitar case and handed it to Zack. "Open it up, Zack. It hasn't been played for years."

He opened the case and found a very good guitar in excellent condition. He removed it from the case and let his fingers strum across it. "This is a very expensive, wonderful guitar. Is it OK if I try to play it?"

"Of course you may. I know it will need tuned and maybe need to be restrung. You may take it home with you, fix it up and enjoy it."

"Wow," he said with a look of pleasure in his eyes. "But what's that?" he said pointing to another case.

"That's my banjo. We used to play together."

"Grandma, these are treasures. Will you play something with me?"

"I don't remember how."

"But will you try?"

"I'll try."

Tom came and stood in the doorway. "Can I pull you two away so we can eat now?" he asked with a smile.

"Grandma and I are going to make music together," Zack told him.

"After we eat," Tom said.

As they put on their coats, Alma felt that she was so happy she could burst. Her eyes fell on the red geranium that sat on the table. She reached out to hold it in her arms for a second.

"Is there a story about the plant?" Mindy asked.

"Yes. It's a magical plant. I know you must think I am daft when I say that but it is magical. It brought its magic power to Bryan, to Pete and Jeannie, and now to me."

Chapter 5
Jeff and Judy

Jeff and Judy were outdoor people. Hiking, camping, backpacking, swimming and skiing were all favorite pastimes for this couple. They both worked at high-powered jobs all week in Philadelphia but on weekends they usually drove to some winter or summer resort in the area to relax. Because of the Christmas holidays they had extra time, so they drove west across the state to a resort they heard was fabulous in the Allegheny Mountains.

Jeff had planned to ice-fish today, and Judy had signed up for figure-skating lessons, but instead they chose to snowshoe across the hills and valleys. This was the first time they had come to this part of the state. The scenery was beautiful so they decided they would explore the area.

After almost two hours of tramping through the countryside they saw what appeared to be a house, sitting on top of one of the mountains.

"Let's go explore," Jeff said and Judy responded, "I'll lead the way."

After about forty-five minutes they came into a yard of a home that had a magnificent view. Jeff and Judy both fell in love with it immediately.

"Do you think anyone is home?" Judy asked Jeff.

"I don't know but let's find out."

They knocked but there was no response. They noticed that there were no tire tracks in the snow that had fallen overnight.

Jeff stood on the porch looking at the beautiful view of the area. "I wonder if this place is for sale," he said quietly.

"Maybe it's just a summer home," Judy said as she poured them hot coffee from the thermos she carried in her backpack along with some snacks the resort had provided. They tramped around the house, looking in the windows.

Jeff sounded so enthusiastic, which was a change from his mood over the past couple of weeks. Judy knew Jeff was very discouraged with his job and was trying to put on a good show that all was well. He had expected to get a promotion to head up a new office in the southwest area of the United States for the environment firm where he worked. But the job had gone to another man. She could understand his disappointment. She, herself, was very bored with her job right now. Sometimes she loved her work, but at times it seemed like a struggle to stay interested.

"Jeff," she said as she put her arms around him, "maybe

this trip happened for a purpose. Maybe we should make some changes. If we could buy this property we could come here year round to enjoy the outdoors and get away from the pressure of work. Or maybe we could get new jobs in this area and stay here all year."

"You know how I love my job in spite of my disappointments," he told her, "but maybe you are right. Even having a place like this to come to would help me keep my priorities straight. Maybe you could even quit your job…"

"And maybe even start a family." Judy looked a bit sad. Their efforts to have a baby had not been successful.

"Let's go back to the resort. Maybe someone there can give us some information on this place," Jeff said as he took her hand.

"Let's take one more walk around the area and then we'll leave."

"Look at that big fireplace in the living room," Jeff said as they looked in the windows. "It covers the whole wall."

"Look at this, Jeff," Judy said looking in another window. "It looks like a second kitchen was built on. There's a big wood-burning cook stove there."

"Amazing," Jeff said. As he turned the corner to the side of the house nearest the driveway he saw something red on the porch that led to the kitchen. "What's that?"

Judy went over to look. "Why, it's a red geranium," she said. "It's very cold out here today but the plant doesn't look too bad. It must not have been here very long. Do you think we should take it with us? I'd hate to see it just sit there and freeze in this weather."

"I have a great idea," Jeff said. "Let's take it with us back to the resort. Tomorrow we will drive to the nearest town and try to find out who owns the property. We can then give the plant to the owner."

Judy unloaded her backpack into Jeff's and put the plant down inside her backpack. It was a very tight fit. But for some reason she wanted it close to her.

When they returned to the resort, Jeff went to the manager and told him about their trip and the house on top of the mountain.

"I think I know the place," he told them. "If it's the one I'm thinking of, you get there from a road out of Zanesville. That town is about a forty-five minute drive from here over the mountain. It you drive over to that area, go to Pete's Grocery store and ask for him. He knows everybody. He'll help you." He reached under the counter and pulled out a roadmap. "I know you probably have GPS in your car but here's an old road map to help you get to Zanesville."

The next morning they both felt very excited about their trip. "I really feel like this might be the start of a new life for us," Judy told Jeff.

"I feel that way too, but we shouldn't get our hopes up. The house may not be for sale. I hope it is. I think we could have a nice home there," Jeff said as he maneuvered the car over the mountain roads.

"I sort of hope no one claims the red geranium," Judy said. "Somehow I feel I want to keep it. But obviously it was left behind by some mistake."

As they arrived in Zanesville they saw a grocery store

with a big sign that said *Pete's Groceries.* "I hope Pete's working today," Jeff said as they got out of the car.

Inside the store it was warm and cozy with the smell of freshly baked bread coming from the oven. The store was decorated for Christmas and most of the employees were wearing Santa hats.

"Welcome to Pete's," a greeter said with a warm handshake. "I don't believe I've seen you here before."

"This is our first time here," Jeff said. "I wonder if Pete is in today. If he is, do you think he'd have time to talk with us?"

"Pete makes time for everyone. I'll page him," she said, and almost instantly Pete appeared with his hand out ready to greet the two visitors.

"Would you possibly have a few minutes to talk with us?"

"Of course," Pete answered. "Let's step into my office and have some coffee."

They introduced themselves, and then Jeff began. "We're vacationing at the Webster Resort over at Fairview. Yesterday we snow-shoed up the mountain. We saw a beautiful home with a million-dollar view. We knocked but there was no one home there. When I asked the manager at the resort about the house, he referred us to you. Do you know anything about the house? We were wondering if the place might be for sale."

"It sounds to me like you are talking about Alma Hartley's place. Did you notice anything special about it or the surrounding area?"

"We looked in the windows. We saw a wall-size fireplace in one room and what looks like a second kitchen."

"Yes," Pete said. "That sounds like Alma's place. Did you say you might want to buy it? Do you have plans for the property? Maybe put in a resort there or something like that?"

"Nothing as elaborate as that. Just a place for us to come to get away from the city and pressures of work," Jeff told him.

"What city do you come from?"

"We work in Philadelphia but our home is west of the city."

"Isn't that pretty far for a weekend visit?" Pete asked.

"We can jump on the turnpike or interstate highway," Judy said. "I really think it would be worth the trip just to have that view. There is something special about the place."

"I agree," Pete answered. "It is special. I know it's not for sale at this time, but the owner is now in her late eighties and lives there alone. She's in Scranton right now spending Christmas with her daughter and her family. I believe she plans to come back to her home. She lives there year-round."

"Then there is no possibility that she would sell?" Jeff asked.

"I can't really say. Her family is anxious to have her move closer to them." Pete paused "Alma may decide she doesn't want to live so isolated from everyone else, but I'm not sure if she is serious about moving right away. Did you say you were up at the house? Did you happen to notice anything unusual around the place?" Pete asked.

Judy spoke up. "We found one thing I thought was very unusual. It was a red geranium on the side porch next to the driveway. I guess it hasn't been too long since Alma left. The plant was still alive."

Pete smiled his biggest smile. "Alma called me the night she left. She set it on the porch by the driveway so no one would forget it. But everyone did forget it. She called and asked me to retrieve it but I forgot until last night. When I got there I couldn't find it. We'll all be happy to know it's safe."

"I brought it with me today. I'll go to the car and get it for you."

"No ma'am, you keep it," Pete said.

"But I can't..." Judy began.

"Let me tell you about that plant. Hear me out before you start to laugh or shake your head and think I'm crazy. That red geranium has magical powers. It has been passed along to at least four people I know, and everyone who has owned it has had something very special and very good happen to them. Alma told me that if I locate the plant I should pass it on to the person who found it. It is my pleasure to tell you that something good is going to happen to you."

Judy saw Pete look at them with a big smile. *Really – magic,* she thought. But wanting to be polite, Judy simply said, "Thank you. I'll take very good care of it. It certainly is a beautiful plant even though it was out in the cold weather for a while."

"Pete, could you do this for us? Could you give Alma our name and phone number and ask her to give us the first chance to buy her property if she decides to sell? I can promise you that we do not plan to do anything to the property except live there. We felt something special there that has been missing from our lives. I think it is just the place for us to get away from the city and keep our priorities in order. Judy and I will take good care of the place. And we'll take good care of the magic geranium," Jeff added with a smile.

"I'll be happy to pass along your information. I hope you'll be patient with Alma. She has lived there many years. This trip is her first off the mountain for a long time. I do believe there is a very good chance she might sell it unless her daughter wants to keep the house."

Judy and Jeff bid Pete goodbye and started back across the mountain. "What do you think?" Judy asked him.

"I'm not sure what to think. Did you believe all that malarkey about the magic of that plant?" he answered her.

"I want to believe it. We're due for a change in our lives," she told him as she reached out to touch the plant.

The next morning they left for home. They carefully secured the geranium so it wouldn't bounce around.

"Well, little red geranium. Do you have some magic for us today or do you have to check us out first?" Jeff asked with a smile in his voice.

"Oh, yes, master. I have all sorts of things planned for you. I might even help you buy a new house," Judy answered in a high squeaky voice.

They both began to laugh.

"Seems like we haven't laughed for a long time. It feels good. We should do it more often," Jeff told her.

"You're so right, Jeff. Between our jobs and our families, I do believe we've forgotten how to smile."

"I promise you, Judy that I will get over this funk about not getting the position at the new office out west. I still have you and a job that I can learn to enjoy again. Let's talk about the house on the mountain."

"Okay, Jeff. And I promise you I will put the idea of having a baby in the back of my mind for a while. We've been so busy thinking about what we didn't have that we forgot to be thankful for what we do have. Do you really think we might have a chance to buy the house? Wouldn't it be wonderful? Can't you just see my mom and dad being there?"

"They'd plant flowers everywhere, trim bushes and clean up the yard even if we told them not to work so hard."

"And can't you just see your mother either being in the yard or on the veranda with her easel and paints. She'd have a whole new world of views to paint."

"Now you're getting me excited. Can't you see us having all our nieces and nephews up for a few days? The kids over ten years old could sleep in sleeping bags or tents and the ones under ten could sleep on cots on the veranda. I bet the sky at night is magnificent. Maybe I could teach them about the stars."

"We could teach them so much – how to identify the different plants and trees."

"I could teach them how to use a compass in the woods."

"I'm sure there is a big pond close by so your dad could teach them to fish," Judy said.

"We've got to get that house, Judy," Jeff told her.

When Judy got home she placed the plant in the center of her kitchen table. Somehow she felt drawn to it with a feeling that she couldn't quite explain. She knew nothing about plants. She had never grown anything. But somehow just touching it made her feel better. *Maybe it's the power of suggestion,* she thought. *I want to believe that it's magic.*

"Looks like we got a ton of missed phone calls," Jeff said as he pushed the 'play' button on the answering machine while Judy started to make coffee.

"Uncle Jeff, this is Robbie. Grandma said you'll be here for dinner on Sunday. Would you please bring your hockey skates? The pond is frozen and I need you to teach me a few new tricks. See you."

"Judy, this is Mom. When you come for dinner on Sunday could you fix your zucchini and tomato casserole? Dad says he's hungry for it."

"Jeff, this is Dad. I've been thinking of taking out an ad for the store in a local paper. What do you think is the best way to get started? Maybe some specials? Think on it and give me a call."

"This is a call for Judy reminding her of her appointment on Friday morning at the dentist office for cleaning and check-up."

"Aunt Judy, this is Cindy. I'm really, really desperate. I need your help. Mom says I'm too young to wear make-up.

Will you please, please call her and tell her I'm old enough? She always listens to you. Bye, bye."

The calls went on and on. Both Jeff and Judy came from large, inclusive families. Jeff had two older brothers and two older sisters. Judy had two older brothers and one older sister. The families were all close. At least once a month each side of the family tried to have a meal for the entire family. The events were always chaotic and noisy but always fun. The families were close and supportive. Both Jeff and Judy were close to all their nieces and nephews.

But sometimes that fact also increased the pain of not having the one thing that was missing from their lives – a child.

They had been eager to have a family from the day they were married. After the first year of their marriage passed and Judy did not become pregnant they both had check-ups at the doctor's office. Judy's monthly cycles were very erratic. A year of treatment with birth control pills had not corrected the problem by the time she stopped taking them. The doctor found no other reason not to have a baby. He told them to be patient. Another year passed. They had more tests. The doctor felt it was just a matter of time since the test results remained the same. Both families knew of their efforts to have a child and were supportive. But as happy as both Jeff and Judy were when nieces and nephews were born there was still an ache in their hearts when a sister or sister-in-law would announce a new pregnancy or when the new baby was born. Jeff and Judy had given passing thoughts to adopting a child but had not seriously looked into how to do it.

When Jeff graduated from college he was hired by a firm interested in the environment, both from the conservation view point and also recycling. Jeff had been a bit surprised when he had received a very nice offer from the environment company. He had not been one of the active protesters on campus, trying to rally everyone around the cause of protecting the environment. But he had studied as much as he could before the interview and became a believer and wanted to do more. He was amazed to find out how many different areas of study were needed to attack the problems requiring conservation – from global warming to local clean water, different laws that govern almost everything and a million new ideas in between.

The firm was not very old but ready to grow rapidly. One of his first assignments had been to work with a committee on a plan to expand the company into the New England area.

The executives discovered that Jeff was a "people" person; one who could easily recognize the strengths of people. He was able to develop those strengths into success. He was detail oriented and had good organization skills. When the opening of the new office in New England had gone smoothly, he was assigned to lead a new project: to plan and open another new office, this time in the southwest area of the United States.

This last year he seemed to make a trip to Phoenix almost every week, trying to oversee the project. In late summer he was asked to provide the names of various candidates to head up the office in Phoenix. Jeff really wanted to head up this office. He felt like it was his baby.

He knew the responsibilities, he had helped write them. He knew the laws that would govern the work, he had to research that aspect to make sure everything complied with the federal and state regulations. Most importantly, he knew the skills required for the office to be successful. He studied long and hard the people who had helped him in the project. There was at least one man whose qualifications stood out, a man named Paul. But Jeff felt like this office was his baby. Jeff had been asked to provide five names of potential managers. He listed Paul's name first but at the very bottom he listed his own name. Surely, he had earned the position. No one knew it better than he. The position went to Paul.

Jeff was very disappointed. Maybe it was time for him to try to move to another company. Of course, if he had gotten the position it would have meant a move out west. What would it have meant for Judy? A change of jobs for her, too? And it would have ended the time they spent with their families.

Judy was an enthusiastic go-getter. She had been a math major in college and said it gave her good training in how to think logically. Now she was IT project manager for a large international communication company. She would be told about a need to update or create a new computer system to make it more effective and efficient. It was Judy's job to determine the best solution, create the plan, calculate the costs and also the savings, develop the system, test it and finally implement it. Judy found her job very tedious but also interesting. She traveled the globe. Most days she enjoyed her job and her co-workers. She worked for a good company. She was also a "people" person and a very caring manager. Her staff and co-workers all loved her. She inspired the people around her to do their best.

Today, she still loved Jeff with the same passion she had felt on their wedding day. It had pained her to see him with such disappointment about his job at this time.

They really did love the life they led. In spite of their desire for a child, they lived a good life. They got up at five each morning and went to the workout room of their condo building. Their condo was small but it was big enough for them.

Judy looked around the living room where she could see the many items they had purchased on her business trips: wood carvings from Africa and Asia, medicine balls from China, decorated eggs from Romania, a leather wall hanging from Nigeria, and so many other items. Every one of the items held a special memory from the countries one or both of them had visited.

They both loved to travel. Often when one was on the road, the other would go to that city for a weekend. They loved to find and explore new places – such as Alma's home in the mountains.

There had been no word from Alma about what they considered their dream vacation home. Jeff thought that maybe he would call Pete someday in the spring. But even if they had bought the house, both of them knew they would have very little time to enjoy it. Still, they really were interested. It might be at the mountain house they would find the magic they needed to feel their lives were complete.

There was one small change in their usual routine after they returned from their trip to the mountains. They developed a game with the red geranium. While having breakfast they might ask the plant if it had a good night's sleep. Judy provided a high squeaky voice for the plant and issued many words of wisdom. They gave it a name one day only to change it the next. Sometimes they would ask it to do a magic trick for them. Judy was sure the plant was smiling at them.

"Maybe this is the magic of the red geranium," Jeff told Judy. "It's like a toy for us to play with."

A week later Judy was sent to Europe by her firm to check on the progress of a new software program the company was hoping to fully implement in the spring. When she got back, Jeff was sent to check the progress of the new office in Phoenix. They were a mobile young business couple always on the go.

After Jeff came back from Phoenix, Judy noticed that his spirits seemed low again. He tried to hide it from her but she could sense something just wasn't right.

"How are things at work since you got back? Anything exciting happening?"

"Everything's okay," he told her.

"You seem a bit down. Are you sure you're okay?"

"It's just that…it's just that I don't think I'm in the loop any more. I used to attend all the meetings of the staff as we planned the new office in Phoenix. I'm told that it's running smoothly. But there seem to be quite a few meetings I'm not informed about. I don't quite know what to make of it."

"Has anyone given you any hints what the meetings are about?"

"No," he told her. "But the entire Board of Directors is in town this week. That's unusual this time of year. Maybe the company is being sold or something. Maybe I should start looking on the internet to see what job might interest me."

"Could you ask someone what's going on?"

"I hate to do that. It sort of lets everyone know I'm not in the loop any more."

"Well, maybe you'll know what's going on soon. Or we could ask the red geranium," she said with a smile trying to lift his spirits.

"What did Pete tell us about it? Something about good things happening in the lives of the owners."

"Well, I'll talk to the geranium tonight and ask it to help us."

"Maybe something good is going to happen on your job," Jeff told her.

"Well, I'm in the boring part of my project. Our new program is being tested in four different countries. So far everything is okay but it's hard to just sit there and wait for the reports to come in."

The next morning Judy got ready for work but instead of hurrying out the door to the office, she sat at the kitchen table looking at the red geranium plant. She felt no energy to get moving.

"Pete told us you were a magic plant. Well, it's time for you to work your magic and get me out of this funk I am feeling," she told the plant. "And it's time you do some magic for Jeff." Then she headed out the door to make her way to the office.

By the time she got to the office she still did not feel quite ready to greet a day of challenges, so she stopped in the cafeteria to get a cup of coffee to take to her desk. Another woman was in line ahead of her.

"Good morning, Judy," the woman said cheerfully.

"Good morning, Maureen," Judy said. "I see you have on another of your beautiful sweaters. Where in the world do you find them? You are famous around here for having so many different kinds and colors."

"You're very kind," Maureen said as she paid for her coffee. "Actually, I make all my sweaters. I started to knit when I was a young girl and never gave it up."

"I'm shocked," Judy said, looking at the woman with astonishment. "I can't believe it. Your work is impeccable. Your blend of colors is fabulous. I've never seen knitting like this. When do you find time to do the knitting when you work so many hours here?"

"I've been widowed for many years. I have just one son. He's in college now. That's why I've been working here. I'm not sure what I'll do now."

"What do you mean?"

"Today is my last day. I made a big goof on a report and they have terminated me. Please don't feel sorry for me. It was my own fault. I used a wrong set of numbers. Maybe my mind was on some new yarn I found on sale at lunchtime that day. I did make a terrible mistake. As sad as I am about losing my job, I really wasn't interested in it. I have a degree in business but working with the routine of paper and computers is just not my thing. Everyone has been very nice to me. Many people tried to cover for me, but my skills and the job just didn't work out," Maureen said.

"What will you do now?" Judy asked.

"I don't know. I admit it will be a worry not to have a regular paycheck. Apparently I didn't worry about it enough to change my ways. But I will find something. I am determined to help my son graduate from the university."

"You should find something that's involved with knitting. Anyone with your talent should stick with it," Judy said.

"I do it for fun and pleasure. I volunteer each Saturday at the Women's Correctional Facility. I take the yarn and knitting needles with me. I'm teaching some of the women to knit. The class is a special privilege given to only a few women. They have to earn the permission to come to class. I have to bring the needles home with me each week so they only get to work on their project for a short period of time. But it seems to be helping the woman and it gives me pleasure. Until I find another job, I'll probably try to go there more often."

"Did you ever think about giving lessons to earn your living?" Judy asked. "I bet the yarn shops would love to have you on staff."

Judy's cell phone rang. She checked it and said she was expected at a meeting. "Maureen, I wish you much happiness. Try to make the most of your talent. I know of no one else who has your skill with knitting needles," Judy said as she left the cafeteria.

Judy's morning was filled with meetings. That afternoon she was knee-deep in paperwork when her cell phone rang. It was the wife of Jeff's boss, Roger.

After a few pleasantries, she asked if Judy could get away from her job to meet her at Jeff's office building.

"I know how busy you are at work and I hate to bother you but my husband asked me to call you. I'm not sure what it's about but I know Roger was not too happy about the year-end bonuses the board of directors authorized. Maybe he got them to change their minds. He sounded very upbeat so it can't be bad news."

Judy said she would be there and left immediately. The women met in the reception lobby. They were directed to go to the auditorium. It appeared the whole staff was there. They were ushered to the front of the area where there were two empty seats in the front row.

Roger nodded to the women and got up to speak. After many introductions were made he acknowledged Paul, the man who had gotten the promotion that Jeff had sought. Roger talked about how much work had gone into this next step of expanding the company, and how sometimes it is hard just to find the right person for the job. Judy prayed for patience and kindness as she sat next to Roger's wife. There were a few announcements made of a routine nature. Finally Roger said he had a major announcement.

"As we start this new year, I am pleased to once more mention all the work that went into opening the new Phoenix office. It went very smoothly and got us off to a good start this new year. The success for this project was achieved by the hard work of one man, Jeff Broder. Jeff, come up and take a bow."

Amid applause, Jeff made his way to the podium and stood next to Roger. Then Roger continued to speak.

"It is my pleasure to announce that our board of directors has authorized me to tell you that a new position has been created: vice president of business development. Our choice for the man for that position is you, Jeff. Your skills at creating and implementing this change in how we use our resources are already reaping benefits for the company. We are pleased to offer you this position. Will you accept these new responsibilities?"

Jeff stood there for a minute in a state of disbelief.

"To say I'm stunned is an understatement. Judy, can you believe this?" he asked as he looked at Judy. Then regaining his composure, he said, "I am pleased to accept your offer." Amid much applause he was escorted to a seat on the podium with the other officers of the company.

Judy sat in the audience, thrilled as she heard the announcement. She knew he could do the job. She knew, through hard work and long hours, he had earned it. Now it made sense why he wasn't offered the job in Phoenix. The management had bigger plans for him. She was so proud of him. Only she had seen his frustrations. *He is a good honest man. They could get no one better for the job*, she thought.

The celebration lasted well into the evening. Finally at last, Jeff and Judy made their way home. As they made their way through the kitchen, Jeff saw the red geranium on the kitchen table.

"Hey, Judy," Jeff said as he reached out to touch the

plant. "Maybe there is magic in this plant after all. I had about given up hope."

Judy laid her hand over his. "I think I can almost feel the energy this plant has," she said as she touched the plant with her other hand. "It reminds me of my Aunt Susie. Geraniums were her favorite plants."

"Call Aunt Susie and tell her your plant can do magic," Jeff said with a smile.

Judy really did hope the magic could extend for just one more task. It was her usual wish. She wished she could get pregnant. Maybe she would make an appointment at the doctor's office tomorrow for one last check-up. After all, the red geranium may have one more magic trick left in it. Her thoughts drifted to the good things she already had in her life. She thought about how lucky she was, having Jeff, and having so many nice things happen. She thought about her desire to have a child. Maybe it is time to think about adoption. Her doctor had told her to take her time when she had expressed her concerns earlier. She was glad that they had waited for both she and Jeff had time to really get to concentrate on their careers and see much of the world together. But now they were ready. If they adopted a child, she could quit her job or at least take a leave of absence. With the salary increase Jeff had gotten with his promotion, she could probably stay home all the time. She knew many women did not have that luxury. She decided she would forget about trying to get pregnant. Instead she would look into adoption.

She thought about Maureen, the sweater lady at work. *She's lost her job; she's trying to help her son through college.*

I bet she's having a bit of a struggle. She apparently had no other source of income. Maureen had said her husband had died years ago. It must have been hard for her to work and try to take care of the boy. Judy hoped that Maureen had been offered a severance package. Then Judy got an idea. She, Judy, wore slacks and sweaters almost every day to work. She would ask Maureen to knit a sweater for her. If it worked out OK then maybe she would ask her to knit a sweater for Jeff. She wanted to help Maureen. As Judy sat there thinking, she had a new idea. She decided that maybe Maureen needed the magic of the red geranium. The magic had already worked for Jeff. As for her hopes, she would try to concentrate on adoption.

One morning the following week Judy called her office and told them she would be coming in a little late. Then she called a friend who worked with Maureen and asked for Maureen's home phone number.

Judy picked up her purse and the red geranium and headed for her car. She entered Maureen's address into her GPS and secured the red geranium in the seat next to her and started off. "Little red geranium, you worked your magic for Jeff and me, so our names can go onto the list that Pete knows about. Jeff is so happy in his job now. He is so good to me and I love him so much. I'm so happy for him. Maureen is a very nice person, always friendly and kind. I want you to work your magic for her. It's not easy to give you up, but I have Jeff to help me. She has no one. So bring her happiness, good health, and success."

A car passed her in the other lane and the passenger looked at her with a weird look on his face. She giggled to herself as she realized he probably saw her talking to the plant. Then she thought of how she had hoped the magic would include a pregnancy. She thought about the many times she was sure she was pregnant only to find out she was not. *Could I possibly be pregnant now? Not very likely,* she thought.

When she was about six car lengths from the corner where she was to make a turn, all the traffic had come to a stop. Nothing moved ahead of her. She was boxed in so had no choice but to sit there. Soon she heard some sirens. She couldn't see anything in front of her. Finally, her lane of traffic started to move, but it moved slowly into a large parking lot where there was a drug store, and then out onto another street. The last time she had visited a drug store was to buy a pregnancy testing kit. That had been months ago. *Could there be any chance I could be pregnant now?* The traffic in the parking lot halted. *Oh, what the heck,* she thought. *I'm stuck here anyway. I might as well go inside and buy another kit.*

Judy pulled into a parking place, got out of the car and entered the store. *I should buy stock in this company,* she thought as she purchased the kit. She got back in her car and found the traffic was now moving slowly again. When she looked toward the corner she saw two cars with dented fenders that had apparently collided there. She continued on her way to Maureen's.

Chapter 6
Maureen

The bedside phone rang early in the morning. Maureen felt no panic at receiving a call so early because she knew that Phil, her son, usually called her when he got off his night shift and was on his way home. She reached for her phone.

"Hi, Mom, did I wake you up? I figured you might be getting ready for work."

"You know I want to hear from you at any hour of the night or day. You must be on your way home. Will you get a chance to get any rest before you have classes?"

"Not this morning, but I did get some shut-eye last night. Some of the trucks got hung-up on the highway so we had some down time." Phil worked nights at a warehouse receiving shipments for a large mega-store. He was a full-time student at the university. Both he and his mother worked very hard to earn enough money to pay his college expenses.

"So tell me, Mom, how are things at work?" Phil asked.

"Things are good. You don't have to worry about me," she told him as she crossed her fingers in the childhood manner of telling a lie. "I had the nicest compliment the other day from one of the bosses. She loves my sweaters."

"Mom, I keep telling you, you should open up your own shop. No one knits as well as you do. When I graduate next year and get a job, my first priority is to buy you a room full of yarn. I'm going to put you there and let you have a picnic."

"I can hardly wait for that day. But tell me, did you get enough hours at work last week to give you some spending money this week or do I need to send you a check?"

"Mom, I'm fine. Take that money and have a night on the town. Maybe you can go to MacDonald's or somewhere special like that," Phil said playfully.

"I think we're running up your phone bill so we'd better say goodbye. Keep safe, son. I love you."

"I love you, too, Mom. Talk with you tomorrow."

Maureen hated lying to her son about her job. Well, she didn't really lie; she just didn't tell him the whole truth about her job. She didn't want him to worry about her. She was concerned about how she would manage financially with no job. Since her husband had died she had managed not to touch her reserve funds, but things cost so much more these days than when she had established the fund. Maybe she should have tried harder to keep her job, but she certainly didn't make the mistake on purpose. The truth was she hated anything to do with computers and paperwork. She loved being creative. She loved interacting with people. But now she needed to find a job. Taxes and insurance still had to be paid. Utility bills came monthly. She tried to be frugal and watch every cent. But her savings had been used for the last tuition bill. She figured her reserve money would only last her about six weeks. She knew she needed to find some source of income. And she needed to do it quickly.

While she was having her first cup of coffee her phone rang again.

"Hello," she answered politely.

"Maureen, this is Judy from the office. Would it be OK if I stop by your place this early? I'm in the car now."

"Of course. Do you know how to get to my home?"

"I have GPS so I'll be there in about ten minutes."

Maureen rinsed her coffee cup and eyed the area to see if it looked presentable. She had some yarns spread out on her sofa and some patterns on the floor but otherwise the room was passably clean.

Maureen opened the door. Judy stepped inside carrying a large potted plant. It was a red geranium. *What is going on?* Maureen wondered.

"I come bearing a gift for you and a request," Judy said.

"Whatever is this?" Maureen asked. "Why it's a beautiful red geranium. Is this for me?"

"This isn't just any red geranium. It's a very special one." Judy told Maureen about her hike in the mountains and finding the plant. "When we went to find the owner, we were told that it was now our plant. Pete said it is a magical plant that lets good things happen to its owner. He said he knew of at least four people whose lives changed after they owned it. I must tell you that now there are at least two more people to add to the list – Jeff and me." She told Maureen about Jeff's good fortune, and added, "I thought about you making some major decisions about your life. I decided you should have the plant. I hope all good fortune will come your way."

"I'm stunned. I don't know what to say." Maureen fingered the leaves of the plant. "I had red geraniums in my yard when I was growing up and even in this house for a time. Are you sure you want to give it up?"

"I'm sure."

"I promise you I will take good care of it. If it truly does work its magic on me, I'll pass it on to someone else. But you said you also have a request for me. What is it?"

"I love that beautiful, shiny, silk and wool sweater you wear. Could you possibly knit a sweater for me? My husband and I both have good high-paying jobs. I can afford any price you want to charge. I do have one request. I have long arms and often the sweaters I buy don't fit me well. Is that a problem?" Judy asked.

"It's not a problem for me. Let me get my tape measure to get some measurements. Do you need it right away?"

"No, because it will be one of those sweaters I can wear year-round forever. It's worth waiting for. But what are all these?" Judy asked, looking at the yarns on the sofa.

"I can't seem to pass up any sale of yarn. I always find a use for it." Maureen paused and then picked up a new pattern lying on the coffee table.

"What do you think of this pattern?" Maureen asked. "I just saw it in a magazine. I hate the colors they used but I have this soft red yarn. What do you think?"

"I think it would be gorgeous. I love the silky shine of the yarn. I think I want one of those sweaters also."

"Let's just start out with the first sweater," Maureen said with a smile in her voice as she started to measure Judy. "If I do a good job for you then we'll talk about another one."

"Have you decided what you're going to do about a job?"

"Are you familiar with Tarrytown?" Maureen asked.

"I certainly am. They have a lot of high-end craft shops there."

"They also have a yarn shop. It used to be very nice but the owner died and the shop has gone downhill ever since. I'm planning to go today to see if I can get a job there. The job may not last long if the shop closes, but it will give me a chance to see if I can do the work. At least I'd be surrounded by something I know about and love."

"Well, I wish you all the best. If it doesn't work out, I bet you could make money making custom sweaters for clients. Please stay in touch and let me know how you're doing."

After Judy left, Maureen stood looking at her yarns and then at the red geranium. "Red Geranium, I could use some of your magic. But maybe it's already working. I've got a job knitting a sweater for Judy. She has lots of friends. Maybe if I do a good job and price it right, her friends will also want sweaters."

About an hour later she arrived in Tarrytown, parked the car in a public lot, and walked to Rosie's Yarn Shop. It was on a street lined with different types of craft shops. She knew that business was always slower during the cold weather but bustled with tourists in the summer. As she neared the store she saw a big sign posted in the window.

HELP WANTED
APPLY INSIDE

She opened the door but saw no one, not even Clair who usually ran the shop. She called out, "Hello – is anyone here?"

"I'll be right out."

Maureen heard the man as he entered the shop from the back room. "May I help you?" he asked politely.

"I want to buy some yarn but I just noticed the sign in your window. Has the position been filled yet? What's happened to Clair?"

"I just put the sign in the window this morning. Clair's been called out of town on a family matter and may not return. I'm Tom Morton and I own the shop. Do you come here often?"

"I've been coming here for years. I love to knit. Clair became a good friend to me. I'll miss her. Do you know if the family matter is serious?"

"Not sure about Clair's family. If you've been coming here for years you probably knew my wife, Rosie."

"Of course. Everyone knew and loved Rosie. We were so afraid you would close the shop after she passed away."

"Well, I almost did, but it seemed like I had a part of Rosie with me when I'd come here to the shop. It was strictly her business and I know nothing about how it operates, but Clair walked me through it. But now Clair is gone, maybe for good. Do you know anything about running a yarn shop?"

"No, but I know almost everything there is to know about yarn and knitting," Maureen told him.

As she spoke, two women customers walked into the store.

"Isn't this charming?" Maureen and Tom heard one customer say.

"Why don't you take off your coat and show me how you handle customers?" Tom suggested.

"Of course."

Maureen dropped her coat on a chair, smoothed her hair and stepped to the front of the store. "Welcome to Rosie's," she said as she offered her hand to the women. "I'm Maureen and I'll be happy to show you our store. Are you shopping or just looking today?"

"I'm shopping for yarn. I love the yarn in your sweater. Did you get it here?" one of the women asked.

"I most certainly did. The yarn for this sweater came from right over here," she said as she led them that way.

Maureen forgot all about Tom. She was in her element. She knew yarns and knitting as well as the different kinds of yarn and the animals that produced the fibers. And she knew how to take care of anything made from any yarn in that store.

The first woman moved from bin to bin, choosing yarn

for this project or that. The second woman was quietly looking on.

"Is there some type of yarn you're interested in?" Maureen asked her.

"I don't know how to knit," she told Maureen. "Hearing you two talk about it makes me wish I knew how. It must be terribly hard."

"It's great therapy for anyone," Maureen told her. "And it's so easy to learn. I'd be happy to teach you."

"Really?" the woman said with enthusiasm. "Where would I have to go to get lessons?"

Maureen felt her stomach slide to her feet. In her enthusiasm to be a good salesperson, had she doomed herself from even getting the job by suggesting something not currently available at the shop? She looked up to see Tom coming from the back room.

"Hello," he said as he shook hands with the customer. "I'm Tom Morton and I own the shop. Did I just hear you inquire about knitting lessons?"

"You certainly did," said the woman. "And this nice lady has said she can teach me. I do hope I won't have to go far from here late in the evening."

"Well, we've been thinking about expanding the shop to create a knitting room for beginners like you."

"You can sign me up. I always wanted to knit an afghan but never could do it."

"Why don't I take your name and phone number and we can get back to you with the details?" Maureen offered.

Maureen helped the women for almost an hour and

made a sale of more than $150. Tom showed her how to ring the sale. She felt good inside as she knew the customers were pleased, but a bit worried that Tom might think she had spent too much time with them or talked too much or failed in some way she didn't know.

After they left, Tom asked her to sit and talk with him, but another customer came in and Maureen left to help the woman.

Tom slipped a note to Maureen saying he was leaving to get coffee and would be back in ten minutes. It made Maureen feel good to think that he trusted her. He came back with two cups of coffee and two bagels.

"Let's sit down and talk," Tom told her as he cleared a corner of the desk he sat behind.

"I guess you really do know about yarns and knitting. You sounded just like my Rosie out there. She had a love for it. I believe you do too."

"I'm sorry I brought up about teaching how to knit," she told him. "Of course you must have your own knitters for that job."

"Well, one thing Rosie taught me was about knowing good knitting from bad. If you really did make the sweater you have on I know you know your business." He paused and then went on. "When we got married, I opened up the Independent Tool and Die Shop out on the highway. I spent all my time trying to get the business established. My Rosie never complained. But she was lonely. None of our family lived in the area and we had no children. She spent a lot of time knitting but had to travel some distance to get her yarn. One day she said she'd like to open her own shop and Rosie's Yarn Shop was born. She had a dream that one day she'd have someone teaching other women how to knit, but she died before we could make it happen. I almost sold the shop several times, but I feel like I'm losing a part of Rosie if I do.

"Clair had worked for Rosie for some years. She was very efficient and nice to the customers, but she had no vision for it. It was a job for her. Something she did well. When she left suddenly a few weeks ago I didn't know what to do. I almost didn't open the store this morning. Then on a whim, I made the sign and put it in the window. I wasn't sure I'd even be open today. It was almost like karma or magic had happened when I heard you greet the customers so warmly."

Maureen said, "I do apologize for bringing up about the lessons. It just popped out. I'm sorry."

"Don't be sorry. It's a great idea. Look at this big room we have back here with just a desk and some boxes in it. We could expand the shop way back here and have you teach knitting in the front window. I bet you could attract other knitters," Tom said. "But I know I'm getting ahead of myself. I'd like to offer you the position if you're interested. We'll need to talk money and benefits. How soon could you start? Do you have to give a notice somewhere else? Do you have family schedules you need to work around? Do you really know how to teach knitting? Rosie always said it took a special talent."

"Tom, I'm very pleased to be offered the job. But you must take at least overnight to think about what you are doing. I finished up working in an office last week so I'm available anytime. I have one son who is a junior at the university and I need a job to help him finish school next year. I have no other family obligations; my husband died when Phil was very young. And yes, I do know how to teach knitting. I volunteer time every Saturday to teach some of the female inmates at the correctional facility how to knit. It's a privilege they have to earn and some of them are doing quite well. Knitting is fun to teach and fun to learn if it's done right. About benefits, I would be willing to take lower wages if I can have health plan benefits. It's quite expensive to buy health insurance on my own."

"I had Clair covered under the blanket of the health plan I use at Independent T & D so that should be no problem," he told her. "But let's both think about it. Can you come back tomorrow?"

"I'll be here at whatever time you say," she told him.

They agreed to meet just before the shop opened at ten a.m.

Maureen almost floated home. She was so happy. To be around other knitters and her beloved yarns was like a dream come true. But could she handle the business end of the shop? If she were to be efficient, she would need to learn new computer programs and finance. She thought she had left the business world behind. Tom had suggested many things in their short time together: she would be in charge of the shop, she would have to decide which yarns to buy, which to put on sale and what prices to charge, and so on and on. Would there also be a remodel of the shop if they decided to teach knitting? Would the teaching be done after or during the hours the shop was open?

Maureen felt like her head was spinning. She thought she wanted to be creative, but was she really ready for a job of this size?

She fixed an early supper since she had skipped lunch, and then got out her skein of yarn and Judy's measurements. She turned on the TV and sat down. As she started to knit she saw the red geranium on the coffee table. *I really didn't believe in magic before but I'm starting to believe it now.*

When the phone rang early the next morning, she knew it was Phil. He was very particular about trying to stay in touch. *But all that will change when he gets a steady girl friend,* she thought with a smile as she picked up the phone.

"Morning, Mom."

"Good morning, my handsome son. Are you on your way to class?"

"Okay, Mom, I know you have good news. What is it?"

"I've been offered a new job."

"At the same place?"

"Actually, it would be managing Rosie's Yarn Shop over in Tarrytown."

"Way to go, Mom! That's wonderful. Did you tell them yes?"

"I'm meeting with the owner this morning. I actually worked there most of yesterday just showing the owner I'm familiar with yarn. We're going to meet this morning to go over a few details."

"You are planning to say yes aren't you?"

"I think I am."

"Mom, I'm at school now. I'll talk to you tonight. Good luck."

Maureen smiled. She was lucky to have such a good son. *He's very understanding and very caring, just like his father,* she thought wistfully.

Maureen put on her pink sweater which had an intricate design in the pattern, and a pair of gray slacks. She took a little extra time with her makeup and left for the meeting with Tom.

He greeted her warmly when she arrived and had coffee and small pastries ready to eat.

"Well, did you decide whether you will come to work here and make this into the best yarn shop in Pennsylvania?"

"Did you decide you wanted a woman who hates computers running your shop?"

"Computers are wonderful," Tom told her with a smile. "We do all our ordering and pay all the bills on the computer. You'll learn our programs in no time, but I'll do it to free up your time at first to make this shop into the best it can be."

They talked for a few minutes about wages and benefits and what hours would be expected of her. They shook hands over the deal. Then he made a request of her. "I'm serious about wanting this shop to be the best it can be. As you learn about our stock and clients, make lists of what changes need to be made to make it top notch. I'm prepared to spend some money to remodel if you think it would help. Look for someone we can hire to replace you during lunchtimes or days off. I certainly don't expect you to spend every minute here. I'll send your name as a contact person to the Chamber of Commerce. They plan many events through the summer that we might want to use to attract customers. For the first three months, I'll take care of office chores, but you must tell me what needs to be done. Do we have a deal?"

"We do indeed," she told him as they shook hands. Feeling very confident, she took the keys from the hanger on the wall and opened the store.

Maureen worked harder the next two weeks than she ever had before. The shop was dusty, new yarn had not been put on display and old yarn was scattered throughout the store. Half empty boxes were shoved into the corner for customers to find. And like-types of yarn were not presented together. When Tom left her alone to go to his office, Maureen didn't know what to do first. She decided would first get rid of the cobwebs and then clean the front windows so that the shop looked welcoming. Many people started to stop by just to see what she was doing. She started to write down her ideas as she thought of them to make Rosie's into the shop she knew it could be. In between she helped customers, both old-time knitters and those who wanted to learn.

By the end of the second week she had ten people signed up for knitting lessons. She and Tom decided that the knitting lessons should not wait until the shop was totally remodeled, so they fixed a section of the back room with tables and chairs, brought in a few lamps for extra light and the lessons began. Tom was anxious to get started on updating the front of the shop, but Maureen persuaded him to wait until she attended the meeting of the Chamber of Commerce.

"They may have a vision for how they want the town to be seen. I think we should cooperate with them for we will certainly benefit if Rosie's is somewhat consistent with their vision."

Tom agreed and soon told Maureen that sales were up enough for her to hire another person full time, so she had time to manage everything else. In less than a month, Maureen's life had changed.

One day as Maureen and Tom worked in the office, she looked up to see Phil coming into the room.

"The woman out front told me I could come on back. Am I interrupting anything important?" Phil asked.

"Phil!" she cried. "What a wonderful surprise. Come and meet Tom who owns this magnificent place." They heard a customer came in the door. "I'll be right back," she told them

"Nice to meet you, Phil. You have a very smart mother. If you're half as smart as she is, you should have a great career ahead," Tom said as they shook hands. "What are you studying at the university?"

"Metallurgical Engineering, sir," Phil answered.

"Did you know that I run a tool and die company here in town?"

"No sir. I thought you owned this shop."

"This was my wife's shop. She died and the shop nearly died along with her. But I had this memory of my Rosie being so happy here and I couldn't bear to close the doors when she died. Your mother came along. She was the right person at the right time to revive Rosie's vision for what the store could become. We are making many plans. Your mother runs the shop and I pay the bills."

"My mother is a very special lady. I'm so glad to see her so happy. It's been a long time since I've seen her smile so much. Look at how much fun she is having helping that customer out front."

"What about you, son? What are your plans?"

"Oh, finish school and hopefully get a decent job."

"Will you be staying at school all summer?"

"That depends on where I find a job. I'm currently working at a warehouse two nights a week and every Saturday or Sunday."

"Have you applied for an internship anywhere? I have just hired a young man for my office for the summer."

"I applied to three places, but I haven't heard yet. I'm still hopeful."

"Where did you apply?"

Phil told him.

"Well, they're all good places. If you are half as smart as your mother, you should do well at any of them."

"Sorry, I was gone so long," Maureen said as she came back into the room. "How long can you stay?" she asked Phil.

"Actually, I'm not staying. The warehouse had a special delivery to be made today. I offered to deliver it so I could get a chance to make sure you're okay, Mom, but I need to get back and hit the books."

"Well, I'm so glad you did. Drive safely. We'll talk tonight."

"You have quite a bright young man there," Tom told her.

"Yes, I do indeed," Maureen said smiling.

When Maureen went home that night she saw the red geranium still on the coffee table. She went over and touched the plant. "Some people might not believe in magic, but I do."

Maureen was very happy over the next few weeks. She loved the shop as if it were her own. She noticed that Tom seemed to spend more and more time there. He was very enthusiastic about her ideas and tried to make sure they were carried out to her satisfaction, yet he rarely left her alone. As far as she knew he was still in charge of Independent Tool and Die Company. She didn't quite know what to think. One day she decided to be brave and confront him about it.

"Tom, I'm so glad you have been able to spend so much time here. Thanks for your patience with teaching me about the computer programs for figuring square footage, setting prices and all the business side of the shop. I do hope you are not letting your time here interfere with your business chores over at Independent."

"Maureen, I must be honest with you. I am almost seventy years old. My business at the shop is well-run by a team of great people. I still have an office, but many times I feel like I'm in the way there. They make good money for me so I shouldn't complain but sometimes I feel they operate better without me looking over their shoulder. But I must be honest with you. You run this shop better than I ever could. I appreciate the way you never complain about my being underfoot all the time."

"Tom, you have been very good to me. And also to my son. Phil called this morning to say he had received an internship for the summer from Acme Tool and Die. The owner mentioned your name. Did you talk with him about Phil?"

Tom was very embarrassed. "I didn't tell him to hire Phil. I just told him Phil's mother is one of the smartest and brightest women I know and if the kid inherited any of her genes, he'd be lucky to have Phil. I would have insisted on hiring him at my place but we had already filled the slot before I met Phil."

"Thank you so much for the recommendation. Phil is thrilled to have the internship. He is a hard-working young man. I don't think he'll let you down."

"Are you getting tired of seeing me around here so much?" he asked her.

"Of course not. It has been so good to have someone as smart as you take over the remodeling and enlargement of the shop."

"Are you aware of how much our sales have increased?"

"Actually, yes, but I didn't know if it met your expectations."

"You have surpassed my expectations by keeping the store open. Anything else was icing on the cake. I kept this shop because it reminded me of my Rosie. But more than that, it gave me something to look forward to each day. Since Rosie died I have been very lonely."

"Do you do any volunteer work in town?"

"No."

"At the last meeting of the Chamber of Commerce

they were looking for someone to oversee the books of the Food Bank and also to help with scheduling at the Women's Shelter. I'm not sure if they pay a salary, but I know they could use your help. And the hospital has a call out for volunteers to help there. There are many jobs of that nature around that can be very fulfilling. Of course, I still need you here too."

"Maybe you are right. I should try to expand my horizons. One smart thing I did was to surround myself by very bright people. My tool and die company doesn't need me and neither do you need me to run this shop. I have the luxury of knowing they are well managed. I reap the rewards without doing any of the work," he said with a smile. "You have given me much to think about."

Maureen now had a staff of five to help in the shop; two-full time and three part-time workers. She had found a very well qualified knitter to help her teach the classes. One of the young women she hired for the evening hours attracted other young women to be interested in knitting. Business was good.

At the shop Maureen researched and ordered yarns made from the wool of many different animals. Some were silky, some had a shine to them, and some were bulky for warmth. Some absorbed the dyes for different colors; some did not. She had been surprised to learn there were so many kinds. Rosie's now carried (or would special order) any type of yarn. Maureen set up a section of the shop with samples of the yarn and an information chart telling about each type of wool.

One project she was considering was the yarn that was

made from the hair of a favorite pet. As a dog would have his hair cut, the hair was saved and made into yarn. Her research showed that it was becoming a popular option for the very rich people who loved their pets. She hoped to have her research completed on the project very soon. She felt it was a chance to make something very special. It could be a way to attract new customers to shop at Rosie's.

With her staff's help, she had also put knitting kits together with yarn and directions for the recreational knitter who wanted to make just a scarf or hat. One proving popular was a kit for a child's hat that looked like an apple. Another popular item was a small afghan for a baby. No serious knitter would look at a kit but beginners were very interested in them.

Maureen worked late every evening on the sweater for Judy. As she worked, she tried to estimate the number of hours she had spent knitting it and the cost of the yarn. Judy had said money was no object but Maureen wanted to be honest about what she would charge. After all, Tom could decide to close Rosie's and Maureen's home knitting could end up being the source of her income. If Rosie's closed she did have some thoughts that she might try to earn a living doing private knitting. But she loved working at Rosie's. She loved the interaction she had every day with people who were becoming her friends and she loved meeting new people. Most of all, she loved to talk about knitting. Of course, if she continued to work at Rosie's she needed to consider whether the money she made from making customized sweaters for individuals should become income for the shop. Should the sweaters carry custom labels saying they were from Rosie's or labels reading they were made by Maureen? She started to laugh. Just a few weeks ago she had been worried about having enough money for groceries and here she was considering a private label.

One evening each month she represented Rosie's when the Chamber of Commerce met. She had surprised herself when she realized that she did have input and knowledge to offer about their various projects to help the town prosper. One night as she went to leave the meeting, Marty Andrews, a local businessman approached her.

"Maureen, you have brought a new enthusiasm to our group. The Chamber is expanding and I sense a new interest in helping it grow. Would you let me buy you a piece of pie and some coffee down at the coffee shop to say thanks?"

"Marty, that sounds wonderful. I skipped lunch today and might even need two pieces of pie."

"Actually, I didn't have lunch either and a burger first with pie for desert sounds very good."

Together they made their way to the corner coffee shop and found a booth.

"Were you always interested in knitting?" he asked her. "You must be aware that your changes at Rosie's are the talk of the town."

"You're kidding me!" she said with a look of astonishment.

"No, I'm not. My daughter asked me if you ever do special knitting. Her sorority at school would like to have sweaters made with their insignia on them. Is this possible?"

"That sounds like a dream job. Tell me about your daughter. You and your wife must be very proud of her."

"She's really special to me. Her mother died a few years ago. It was hard when Amy went away to school. She felt she needed to stay home to take care of me. But I want her to be able to take care of herself. She had a good first year at the university and stayed on campus this summer to help with a summer camp for under-privileged kids. But I talk too much. Tell me about you. Do you have children at home?"

"Just one. My husband died in an accident when our son was just two years old. He is a wonderful young man and a very good son. He is studying metallurgy and has an internship this summer. He plans to graduate in the spring."

"You never re-married?"

"No," she said quietly and then said, "Tell me about your wife."

"She died from cancer when our daughter was fourteen."

"Life is not always easy for any of us," Maureen said quietly.

Their friendly waitress appeared at their side, pouring more coffee into their cups. "Are you ready for another sandwich or at least a piece of pie? You know we're famous for our pies."

Marty spoke. "Actually, that's why we came."

"The burger was great," Maureen said, "but I think I'm much too full to have pie."

"Then why don't I take one super-sized slice and cut it into two pieces. It will be just big enough to satisfy your sweet tooth. We have a great banana cream pie and fresh cherry pies that will make you want more."

They agreed on the cherry pie.

After dessert, Marty walked her to her car. Maureen turned to him. "This has been so much fun. Thank you for asking me."

"Thank you for saying yes. Sometimes the evenings get very long."

"I know exactly what you mean," she said quietly.

"There's a concert in the park on Friday night. Would you be interested in going to hear a couple of local bands?"

"I'd like that a lot," she answered.

As she turned on the lights at home she felt a sense of pleasure and happiness that was rare since her husband had died. Finally, she knew she could take care of herself. She was grateful for the friendships she was making. She picked up the picture of her late husband that she kept on her nightstand. For the first time since he had died she felt certain that she would be able to make a life without him. Tom was generous with the salary he paid her. She was able to pay her bills and still have some money in the bank. She looked at herself in the mirror. She saw brown hair and big brown eyes. She even thought her skin had a fresher look to it. Maybe it was because she was smiling more. Finally, she was beginning to love life again. She loved working at Rosie's. She felt confident that she could now support herself and her son.

One evening she held up the sweater she had made for Judy and decided it was perfect. She called Judy and suggested she stop by to try on the sweater to be sure the sleeves were the right length.

Judy was very happy to get the call and was thrilled with the fit of the sweater after trying it on. She was also anxious for Maureen to get started on the second sweater of the soft red yarn she had seen the first day.

"You look very content," Judy said. "Were you able to locate another position?"

Maureen was very happy to update Judy about her success in managing Rosie's. Then she paused and very pensively asked Judy, "Do you think it is the magic of the red geranium?"

"I never thought I'd say I believe in magic but I do believe in that red plant. It's still working its magic. For so long I had wanted to become pregnant, and now I am. We are so happy to be having this baby. And the doctor said I am fine and everything is going well."

"I'm so happy for you! I'll knit something special for the baby. And I have to thank you for giving me the red geranium. It has certainly worked for me. I have never been this happy in a job. It was the right place at the right time."

Tom came into the store a few days later with the news that he had made a decision. Unofficially, he was going to retire from Independent and spend less time at Rosie's. He was going to try to become a professional volunteer.

He had decided he needed to get involved in something he cared about. He wasn't sure what that would be, but wanted to give it a good try. Maureen was pleased, but warned him not to get so involved he would forget that she still needed him to help her at Rosie's. She was a bit concerned for Tom. In many ways he seemed so sad and lonely. She hoped he would follow through on his thoughts about becoming a volunteer. It might help him make new friends. Even when she was home she worried about him.

Then Maureen had a new idea. She walked to the red geranium on the table and began to speak aloud. "You worked your magic for me. I can't remember when I have felt this good. I love working at Rosie's. I love the people I work with and the customers I meet. I love being able to look at my son without worrying about getting through the next week. And I enjoy my friendship with Marty. It's nice to be able to talk about your day with someone special. But I think it's time I pass you on. I'm going to give you to Tom. I hope you have some magic left for him. He is a good man. I want him to have a happy life."

That same morning she took the plant with her to work.

"What's that?" Tom asked as she placed the plant on the window sill next to his desk.

"It's a magic red geranium. Don't you laugh at me, Tom. This plant was given to me the morning of the day I came here looking for yarn. I had lost my job and I was feeling very desperate. You gave me a job and I love what I'm doing. I want to make this shop the most outstanding yarn shop in the country. Thank you so much for helping me find my way."

"I should thank you. Rosie would be so pleased if she could see how successful the shop has become. I was just looking over last month's figures. We've never had a month like that before."

"I'm glad about that but I want you to have this plant so it can work its magic to help you find happiness in your personal life."

Tom spoke quietly. "Thank you, Maureen, but I'm a bit old for that."

"Indeed you are not. Let's just wait and see how this plant will change your life."

"You really think it will?"

"I really think it will."

CHAPTER 7
TOM

A few days later Tom was paying bills at one desk and Maureen was ordering supplies at another. They heard the door of the shop open and heard Angie, one of their sales reps, greet the customer. Then they heard a loud laughing voice say, "You don't have to help me, honey. I used to run this shop. Is Tom around?"

Tom said, "That sounds like Clair. I didn't know she was back in town." Clair was the woman who ran the shop after Rosie died: the person Maureen had replaced. "Don't bother to get him," they heard her say. "I'll just go to the back room and find him myself."

Tom had started to rise from his chair when Clair came into the room.

"Tom, Tom, darling. It's so good to see you again. I've missed you." She rushed to him and gave him a big hug and a kiss on the cheek. She gave Maureen a passing glance but kept her eyes on Tom as she spoke. "Hello, Maureen.

I heard you are in charge here now and making many changes. How sweet of you to help Tom."

Tom stood there, staring in amazement at the woman who entered his office. "Clair?... Clair?... is it really you?" he asked.

"Oh course, darling. It's your Clair coming back to see you."

"Clair, I would have passed you on the street and never recognized you. You have changed everything about yourself. What have you done? What's going on?" Tom asked.

"Well, I left here because my brother was dying. He passed soon after I got to California. He never married, just like I didn't. We both preferred to play the field. My brother accumulated a fortune and left it all to me. When I found out how much money I had, I decided to get a complete makeover. I think it came out pretty good, don't you?" Clair asked as she turned very slowly in front of him.

"I've never seen you look like this," Tom said.

"Yes, I know, darling. It's quite a change."

Standing before him was a blonde woman, dressed in a very expensive black suit, wearing five-inch heels, carrying a bag that must have cost at least $700. Her make-up was done so perfectly it appeared she had none on, yet no one has such flawless skin naturally. She had enough gold necklaces around her neck and bracelets on both arms to sink a battleship, and big flashy rings on her very long, brightly painted fingernails. Tom simply could not recognize her as the same woman who had worked in the shop for years. He didn't want to stare but he couldn't take his eyes off this woman. The last time he had seen Clair, her hair had been a mousey gray with a few dark streaks that was pulled over to one side and held with a bobby pin. He had never seen her wear anything but dark brown slacks with a short-sleeved polyester shirt. She always wore bedroom slippers at work. She never wore any make-up, not even a touch of lipstick. Rosie always had to insist that Clair greet the customers and try to be friendly but Clair had been very shy and found it hard to look people in the eyes. But now, when she talked, Clair made big gestures with her hands and arms. She laughed long and loud and flirted with Tom. How could this be the same woman?

"I found a marvelous plastic surgeon in L.A. who worked a lot of magic on me." Clair caught a glimpse of herself in a mirror and reached to touch her hair. "He did a few nips and tucks here and there on my body. He was marvelous, darling." She looked at Maureen. "I'll be glad to give you his name if you're interested," she told her. Without waiting for an answer Clair continued. "Then I went to a good hair salon." She lifted her chin and shook her golden hair slightly. "Is it true, Tom, that men really do prefer blondes? I think it must be, because I've had a very big social life since I became a blonde."

Tom stood there stunned. He noticed that Angie and two regular customers were standing near the doorway to the office trying to sneak peeks of Clair. He looked at Maureen who tactfully turned to Tom and Clair, and said, "Excuse me. I believe they need help out front."

Clair reached out and closed the door as Maureen left the office.

"Darling, darling Tom. I've missed you so much."

"Well, we missed you around here. I knew you needed to be with your brother but I wasn't sure what to do about the shop."

"Well, I'm glad you found Maureen. This shop needed someone like her, someone who knows and appreciates knitting. Heaven knows I never learned. I just was never interested in it. But I did like Rosie and I certainly did like you. Looks like you've changed things around quite a bit."

"I let Maureen make all the decisions now."

"And I bet it's making a profit. Oh, well, so much about the shop. Tell me about you, Tom darling. Have you met someone special yet? Did you get married while I was gone?"

"No, of course not. I don't have time. The plant and the shop keep me busy."

"Well, you know what they say about all work and no play. Why don't we go out for coffee so we can have a comfortable place to sit and talk and get caught up on all the news?"

"Well, I guess we could do that," Tom said slowly. "I can't believe how you've changed. I bet no one recognizes you."

When Clair and Tom came out of the office, she was holding tightly onto Tom's arm.

"Now you people are just going to have to work a little harder on your own. I'm taking Tom out for coffee and we may not come back all day," Clair announced.

Tom looked like he was in a daze. He was completely mesmerized by this woman who had invaded his life.

They didn't return to the store until it was nearly closing time. They walked in the door and Clair reached over and kissed him on the cheek. "Bye, bye, you sweet man. I'll see you tomorrow morning," she told Tom.

In a shaking voice Tom announced they planned to spend the next day touring Philadelphia. Then for a moment he regained some of his professional persona. "That is, if you think you can manage without me here," he said to Maureen.

"I think we can manage OK," she told him. "I hope you will have a pleasant day on your trip."

"Clair's really changed."

"She certainly has."

"Maureen?"

"Yes?"

"She wants me to wear a pair of white slacks, a navy blue blazer and a shirt with no tie."

"That would look very classy. Do you have white slacks?"

"No."

"Why not wear gray or khaki slacks? I think either would look very appropriate this time of year."

"I think I'll go home and see what I got in the closet. Clair thinks I should dye my hair. What do you think?"

"Do what makes you happy," Maureen said, trying not to smile.

"I just thought of something," he said.

"What's that?"

"Do you think the red geranium is working?"

Maureen gulped long and hard and then told him she didn't have the slightest idea.

Clair drove up the next morning around ten o'clock. She was driving a new red Mustang convertible that had every possible accessory on it. Tom had to admit it was a very flashy car. Clair put the top down as Tom got in and drove off with great authority at a high rate of speed.

"I seem to remember you used to take the bus to work. When did you learn to drive?" he asked her.

"While I was in L.A. Everyone out there drives. The first time I was on the expressway I was scared but very soon I drove the same way they did. It's very exhilarating to drive with authority."

As soon as she entered the expressway she increased her speed and they reached downtown Philadelphia very quickly. "What do you want to see first?" she asked Tom as they got out of the car.

Tom was shaking a little. He had never reached Philly in so little time. But he regained his composure quickly by deciding he wanted to have some control over how they spent the day. He suggested they take a professional city tour so they didn't miss any new places. In the morning they visited the Franklin Institute and Independence Hall. At lunch time they ate the famous cheese steak sandwiches at the new Franklin Square Carousel and visited the new Liberty Bell Center to see the new home for the Liberty Bell. They visited the Museum of Art, and several new shops offering evidence of how Philadelphia has changed over the years.

As they left the bus after their final stop, Tom said, "The bus driver's suggestion that we might want to take the early dinner cruise on the waterfront sounds good to me. What do you think?" he asked her.

"I think it sounds wonderful. Let's go."

Some three relaxing hours later, they returned to her car for the trip home.

"This has been the very best day of my life," Clair told Tom. "I can't remember ever having so special a day. Thank you so much."

"Clair, we've know each other for years. But I saw a new you today. And I have to admit I can't remember laughing this much for years."

"You were a very true, loyal husband to Rosie for many, many years. I think she would be happy to see you laugh a little." She paused and then reached out her hand, "Goodnight, Tom," she said quietly.

As he shook hands with her he placed his left hand over hers. "Thank you for a wonderful day. I'll call you tomorrow."

Tom slept late the next morning. It was nearly noon when he awakened. He drank his coffee, ate his bowl of cereal and remembered every detail of the prior day. Then he remembered Rosie's. This was the first time he had missed being at the store in the morning. He thought he should phone the shop, but decided they could manage just fine without him. Someone might ask questions about his day yesterday and he didn't want to share the details with anyone.

He paced around the house for the next couple of

hours, listening to some news on TV and reading the morning paper. Finally, he decided that he might as well stop fighting his feelings. He wanted to see Clair again. He phoned the hotel where she had taken a suite and asked to be connected to her room. There was no answer. Finally the receptionist told him Clair might be in the fitness room as the operator knew she worked out each day. Tom decided to leave a message asking her to call. Then he began pacing the floor again, waiting for the phone to ring. It did a few minutes later.

"Tom, I got your message. Is everything okay?" Clair asked a few minutes later.

"It's fine. I just thought I'd call to see if you survived yesterday."

"I had a wonderful day. Are you at the office? At Rosie's?"

"No, I don't think they need me at either place every day. I guess I've been going in regularly because I have been lonely."

There was a long pause as neither of them said anything. Then Clair asked, "Do you work out every day? They have wonderful fitness facilities here at the hotel. I have just been doing my daily work-out."

"Maybe I should join a gym," Tom said. "Or maybe I'm too old. You young chicks would have a good laugh if I worked out."

"Don't be silly, Tom. Everyone needs to exercise." She got very quiet for a moment and then said, "When I arrived in L.A. my brother was already in a hospice. He was asleep when I got there so I sat quietly in a chair. When he woke he was glad to see me, but said for a moment he thought I was my mother sitting in the chair. He said I looked just like her before she died. She was in her nineties. He told me I must change how I live; that I was too young to give up on life. From his dying bed he called his trainer and asked him to take me on as a client. That was the start of my transformation. After I joined the gym, I learned to drive a car. And if you've ever driven on the L.A. expressways and survived, you will have earned all sorts of confidence for building a new life. I was so fortunate that my brother left me enough money to make the change with expert help. I'll admit it. I do enjoy spending his money."

"Well, the change is wonderful. I think your personality was hiding deep within you. I was just wondering if you'd like to go to dinner tonight. There's a new Chinese restaurant that opened out on the highway. I have been wanting to try the food there. Do you already have plans for tonight or could I pick you up about six?"

" I'd love that."

"I don't know what to wear," he admitted.

"Anything casual would be fine, I'm sure."

"I don't know what casual means."

"Just a shirt without a tie will be fine."

"I'll see you at six."

"When she got into his car that evening he asked, "Do I look OK?"

"You look very nice," she told him.

"This red flowered shirt isn't too loud? It's probably the most casual shirt I own."

"You're a handsome man, Tom. You would look good in

anything. The shirt is a little dated. Would you like me to take you shopping tomorrow for some updated clothes?"

"That probably would be a good idea. Do you have time?"

"You forget something, Tom. I'm a wealthy woman. My time is my own. I think it would be fun for us to have a shopping trip tomorrow. I want to give you my cell phone number so you can reach me easily. Is it OK for me to have your cell phone number?"

"I don't have a cell phone."

"Everyone has a cell phone these days."

"Well, I don't."

"Then that's another thing we can shop for tomorrow. Let's plan to meet early, around ten or eleven, then we can shop, have lunch, and then shop some more."

Tom smiled. "That sounds like a good plan to me."

The next morning he answered the doorbell and found Clair on his doorstep. "I just thought that if we're going to shop for clothes, I should see what's in your closet. Is it OK if I peek in there?"

"That probably makes a lot of sense. But I'm embarrassed for you to see the inside of my house. I have a housekeeper come in once a week to clean, but suddenly everything looks shabby to me."

Clair just laughed and with a wave of her hand said, "Oh that's all easy enough to change. But today we'll just start with your clothes. Why not open the shades so we can see the colors in a natural light?"

Clair began to sort through his clothes. "Those wide lapels on some of your jackets have been out of style for ten years or more. You must have been very heavy when you bought those. Those must be things you bought when you were on vacation," she said looking at another stack of shirts.

Tom didn't quite know what to think. It appeared he had very little left in his closet. Of course, if he was honest, he would have to admit he had bought not one new item since Rosie had died and that was almost eight years ago. He did see Clair toss a couple of favorite shirts he might have to rescue. But Clair had other ideas. She had him bring her some big plastic bags and then proceeded to fill them with his clothes. "That suit must be very old. Do you remember when you got it?" she asked him as she found another suit in his closet.

"I got that suit and the gray one at Alfred's."

"Alfred's? They've been out of business for twenty or thirty years. Oh, dear, we have a lot of work to do. If we have no luck today, we'll take some of your old clothes back out of the bag. But I think we are going to have a wonderful day," she told him with a toss of her head and a blinding smile.

And they did. He got a new suit, a high-priced classic one, two sports jackets, and slacks, shirts, knit tops, a casual jacket and a couple of sweaters Clair had a very critical eye for fit, and insisted some had to be tailored. She even made him buy a couple pair of jeans and sweat shirts. They also shopped for a pair of dress shoes, a pair of loafers and some athletic shoes for casual walking. He got a sweat suit to wear to the gym. He felt like a little boy on Christmas morning when he got home that evening and put his new clothes in the closet. He carefully laid out all the sales slips on his dresser as he hung his clothes in the closet. Now he looked at the slips carefully, added them up and smiled. "It's a small price to pay to look so good," he told himself as he looked in the mirror.

The next morning Tom bounced out of bed, did a few stretching motions and vowed to start a real exercise program the next day. He turned on his radio and found some music to listen to instead of the news. He showered and shaved and feeling very adventurous, removed his new jeans from the closet along with a blue knit shirt that Clair had told him matched his eyes.

He decided he had to get a different hair style. Maybe the stylist Clair had told him about could cut his hair for him. He put on the new pair of athletic shoes and decided he was set for the day. The new clothes felt strange in one way, but also made him feel ten years younger. Now maybe he wouldn't stand out on the streets as an old man. Instead of his usual bowl of cereal which he thought was good for his digestive system, he decided to stop for a latte and maybe a bagel.

He had become a new man. He made his way to Rosie's. These 48 hours away from the shop was the first time he had not been there each day.

"Good morning," he said cheerfully as he opened the door some ninety minutes later than he usually arrived. "Did you miss me the past couple of days?"

"Well, good morning, Tom," Maureen said quickly as she came out of the office. "You look really special today. Did you have a good couple of days off?"

"I had a wonderful couple of days," Tom said. "Angie, you look like you're going to explode. You can go ahead and laugh if you want. I know I look different. But you are looking at the new me. I gave away all my old clothes and now I'm going to try to dress more appropriately."

"Sorry, Tom, I hope I didn't offend you. I just wasn't sure it was you when you walked in the door," Angie said looking very embarrassed. "You look really, really good. You look twenty years younger. I love your blue shirt. It's the same shade as your eyes. I had never noticed how blue they were before."

"Well, it was time for a change for me. Now tell me what is happening around here."

Tom checked some mail, paid a couple of bills and checked on the status of the remodeling plans of the shop. He actually came out of the office twice to talk to a couple of customers about their knitting. Then he left for lunch with Clair and said he might or might not be back to work. It made him feel very good to say this for it meant he had other things in his life that he could do instead of just work, work, and work.

One day Tom was standing with his hand on the red geranium when Maureen walked into the office. He smiled at Maureen. "You told me this plant had magical powers. I believe it does. You might think I'm an old man into his second childhood, but I feel more alive and useful than I have for years."

"Tom, I'm glad that you are able to have more pleasure in your life. I could tell how lonely you have been. Since

Clair came to town you have a new vitality in your step and a broad smile on your face. I want you to be happy."

"Did you worry that Clair might want to come back to the shop?"

"Maybe, right at first. But I think Clair has found a new way of life. She has so much energy and enthusiasm for living. I don't think I really knew Clair at all."

"None of us did. Her brother changed her life, not only by leaving her money, but by insisting she start to get a life. His money made it a little easier for her to make the change. She has no relatives or close friends. Her life had existed in coming to this store to work every day. Now she's full of energy. We're going down to the mission to help feed the homeless today. Which reminds me, I'm late picking her up. I'll see you later."

Tom was surprised when he and Clair got to the parking lot of the mission. Although lunch would not be served for almost another hour, already a line had formed. He saw mothers and fathers, old and young people, people dressed neatly and people in very tattered clothing. He felt a little embarrassed but more chagrined to see such a crowd in his own town. He knew there were needy people but in his mind he thought maybe there were only a dozen or so. He felt a wave of empathy go over him. He wondered if anyone in the line was someone who had been laid off by his tool and die company. Though he hadn't gone to the office regularly the last year, he knew there had been lay-offs during that time.

Today's menu at the mission featured spaghetti. Tom was told that the different churches in the area took turns supplying meat and the rest of the food was donated. The cooks never planned the menu until they had a chance to see what came in that day. Tom and Clair were put to work cleaning the vegetables that were to be used in a salad. Some of the produce was donated because it was old, so they took care to use only the best part of the vegetables. It was a true learning experience for Tom. The experience made him realize how much of a loner he had become. He did not really see the world around him. He felt he had to do more. There were always requests for money in his mail, but had he ever stopped to consider who the money was helping? He was very quiet as he worked and the quietness continued when he and Clair left the mission.

"I've heard of missions all my life but this is the first time I have visited one. I'm glad you brought me here today. Thank you, Clair, for helping me to see the life around me. I guess I buried my head in the sand and busied myself either at the tool shop or Rosie's. I have the means to do more. I should do more."

"Tom, you are a good man. I know you'll do the right thing when you feel the time is right," Clair said lovingly.

"I was surprised to see so many people here."

"There's always been a crowd here. My mother and I used to come here regularly until Rosie gave me a job at the yarn shop."

"Clair, I had no idea. How did you get together with Rosie?"

"It was at the Thanksgiving dinner given by the churches. You and Rosie were both working there. She sat down to talk with me and learned I needed a job to support myself and my mother. She offered me a job at the shop. I knew I wasn't really qualified but I tried my best."

"Rosie loved and respected you. I had no idea that's how you met. But I don't understand something. If your brother had so much money why didn't he try to help his mother and sister?"

"It's a long sordid story but I'll give you the short version. My brother was really the son of my father and his lover. My mother never forgave my father for having an affair and refused to have anything to do with her step-son. My brother was quite a bit older than me and never seemed to need money. I was never allowed to accept any presents from him. My mom and I struggled financially until I got the permanent job at Rosie's. After my mother died and I went through her things, I found many letters, most with checks still in the envelopes that had not been cashed, that my brother sent to help us. When I heard he was dying, I knew I had to go to him. He was very gracious and I believe a very good man. But he didn't want me to save the money he was leaving to me; he wanted me to spend it. And his friends rallied around me to help me change my life."

It was hard to stay depressed when one was around Clair. She constantly had new ideas on how to have fun. For instance, she had gotten them both memberships at the local health club. Now they both went each day to meet with a trainer who had a different program for each of them. Tom began to feel great and have more energy when he worked out every day and ate a larger variety of food. One day Clair announced that she was going to enroll them for dance classes.

"Now I think you are going too far," Tom told her.

"Nonsense," Clair said. "You are going to be the master of the Latin dances."

"No way, no way, I'm going to do that," he told her sternly.

"We'll see," she said with a smile.

A few days later Clair announced that she was going to shop for a condo. There were new units being built and she wanted to see them so Tom went with her. The new units were another eye-opener for Tom. He had no idea such luxury was being built into them. When he went back to his house, he saw the over-grown bushes and trees and a house that needed a new coat of paint. The inside of his house looked really old and dingy. He thought a lot about how Rosie had kept after him about the upkeep of the house, but after she died he did absolutely nothing except exist there.

He decided to take a walk around the neighborhood, something he had not done for years. When he and Rosie moved in they had known everyone. The families got together often. As he made his way around the block he realized he did not know another family. Almost all of the homes had beautiful lawns, and nice landscaping. They looked like good family homes. He saw a few neighbors who greeted him warmly. *I bet they hate me for not keeping my property in better shape.* When he arrived back home he took a good look at his house. The bushes and trees were so overgrown you could barely see the house from the street. There were no neatly trimmed bushes or colorful flowers blooming. Instead he saw bare patches of earth where Rosie had planted her flower gardens: pansies in the spring, impatiens and begonias in the summer and chrysanthemums in the fall. He sat on the porch step and wondered where the years had gone. He wondered how different things might have been if Rosie had lived. She was the social butterfly in the family. He always kept his mind on his work. He shook his head. *Where had the years gone?*

Tom realized that Clair had opened a new door for him. He decided he would walk through. Already he felt much younger than he had in years. The workouts and new interests he was enjoying made him feel he did still have a life ahead of him.

Tom pulled his new cell phone from his pocket and called Clair. "It's OK, Clair. Sign us up for the dance lessons." Then he called a local landscaper. "Send someone out to help me find my house in this jungle."

The instructors at the dance studio were superb. Tom felt embarrassed that he didn't seem to be able to count 1-2-3 or 1-2-3-4 but the woman instructor kept encouraging him and telling him he was doing great. He had one moment that first evening when he felt like he was really feeling the rhythm of the music. He and Clair made plans to practice together during the week and come back the next week for lesson two. Tom took to the dancing a lot more quickly than he thought possible. Tom's whole demeanor changed. No longer did he feel like an old man walking down the street. Now he felt like a suave man walking with a purpose. Though he did not agree to dye his hair, the new shorter cut given him by the stylist made him feel and look years younger.

Prior to his transformation, Tom had just about given up stopping by Independent T & D, the company he owned. Now when he stopped by he acted like an owner. He asked for certain reports and wanted to be updated about business. He was no longer the mousy little man at Rosie's. He chatted with the customers, asked for sales numbers, made additional suggestions for the renovation taking place there. Tom was a man enjoying his life.

"Hello, you beautiful little red geranium," he said one day when he came into the office. "You did change my life."

Tom had never taken time for any hobbies or sports but he discovered a love for dancing. Clair had been right when she said he had a talent for the Latin dances. He felt as if he had Latin blood in his veins. Clair preferred some of the more traditional dances. They continued to practice every day. Their instructors were very pleased and invited them to join a group of beginning dancers that met twice a month, just to dance with each other and have fun.

Both Tom and Clair loved to dance. Clair was a natural as she floated on Tom's arm, bending this way and that to give grace to their movements. What Tom lacked in natural ability he made up for in practice. He walked around his house with his shoulders back. He practiced twirls and bends. He even tried some hip-hop in the privacy of his own home. He found a new passion.

Tom had practically no time in his life for Independent T & D or Rosie's. One day he stopped by to see Maureen.

Instead of the little Victorian shop with a dusty look to it, the remodel had been completed. He recognized that Maureen's vision for the store had been the right one. The store still had Victorian charm but with a new up-to-date décor. It looked wonderful. Maureen proudly sat with him at the computer while they went over the financial reports. The store was making higher profits than it had ever made.

Maureen took this opportunity to explain to Tom about the sweaters she was knitting on her own. She thought it was time she had a label for her sweaters since she now had orders for seven sweaters, mostly from friends of Judy. She asked him what kind of label she should use. She told him she felt that she should use one with the name of Rosie on it. She said she would not feel comfortable doing so without Tom's blessing. Tom was a little surprised by her words but asked her many pointed questions: how many hours did she spend on a sweater, what was the cost of the yarn she used, what did she charge for the finished sweater. He then asked her for a few days to think about it and consult his attorney. The next week he called and asked Maureen to meet him at a restaurant for lunch for a business meeting. Tom's attorney was there also.

The attorney had been hard at work. "Tom has told me so many good things about you. Knowing what Tom would like to do, I looked into your background and your knitting history. My research has shown that you have a fan. This fan has shown your skills to a well-known fashion designer in New York. This designer is considering using one of your sweaters in his next fall fashion show. It may not happen but you should be ready with a response in case it does."

Tom looked at Maureen who sat there in a daze. She said nothing.

"Can we keep talking or do you need time to recover?" Tom asked with a smile on his face.

"I don't know what to say," she finally mumbled. "It's only been a few months since I didn't have a job."

"Well, we need no answers today," the attorney said. "Tom has a proposal for you. He is willing to invest in a new business, *Sweaters by Maureen*, or some such name. But at least for the present time, he needs you to manage and oversee Rosie's Yarn Shop."

"Maureen," Tom said quietly, "You rescued Rosie's for me. I will always have a special place in my heart for the shop. But I think you are destined for bigger things. I am willing to invest in you, whatever money it may take, to get your own business started. As for Rosie's, well, you rescued it from oblivion and made it into a viable business. I don't want to lose it but I don't have the skills to take it forward. You always have so many good ideas. If you could still find time to over-see the shop for six months or a year, I would be very grateful. We will find someone special to manage the shop on a daily basis to free up your time. But you must think about your future. The time for you to shine is now."

"Tom, you are so good to me. I don't know what to say," she said as she sat there, still in a daze.

"Talk it over with your son. He is a bright young man with a good head on his shoulders." And then with a smile he said, "You can talk it over with the red geranium when you're in the office. It certainly has worked its magic for both of us."

That evening Tom and Clair had dinner together and then left for their dance lesson.

"Tom, you look like the cat that ate the canary. What's up?" Clair asked.

Tom told her of his plans to help Maureen.

"Does this mean she gets the red geranium back?" she asked with a smile.

"Nope, when I give it away it will be someone new. Maureen had her turn with it and that crazy little plant was good for her and good for me."

They both sat deep in thought as they drove along.

"How about our dance instructors, Linda and Dan? They survived that terrible accident that caused them to change their careers. After having been on the stage on Broadway, it must have been devastating to know their dream of being big stars was gone. They can't be making very much money with the dance classes they teach. I know the old farm that belonged to his family. It really needs a lot of work done on it."

"Aren't we close by the farm now? I don't believe I know exactly where it is."

"Turn left at the next intersection. I know the farm well. Dan's grandparents were very kind and gentle people. Everyone loved them. Their farm is the next place on the left."

Tom drove slowly by the property. It did not look like a farm. They saw what almost appeared to be an overgrown field. A house sat in the center. But even though the house was in dire need of paint, they could see the touches Linda and Dan had made. The grass surrounding the house had been cut and the front porch looked very inviting with cushions on the swing and in two chairs and a collection of corn stalks and pumpkins placed in one corner. The driveway and walk to the garage looked neat.

"It looks pretty nice, but somehow my eyes are drawn to the need for paint, repair to the siding and a new roof. It will take a lot of money to restore it," Tom said.

"They can't be making very much money from the dance studio," Clair said. "I heard rumors at the gym that they are considering closing it."

They drove quietly for a few minutes. Then Tom turned to Clair.

"Clair, my dear, you really are brilliant. They do need the luck of the red geranium. Let's stop by Rosie's to pick it up and I'll take it to them tonight."

CHAPTER 8
LINDA AND DAN

Linda looked around the room trying to make sure it was clean and ready for the adults who would be coming for the ballroom dance class. This afternoon it had been filled with fifteen tweens and teens who were learning ballet. Things often got left behind. Linda put a note on the items with the date and take them to a special shelf. She decided the room looked as good as she could make it. It definitely did not meet her standards but it was the best she could do. "Do you have the music set?" she asked Dan.

"I think so," he told her. "Is there anything special we should play tonight?"

"I guess not."

She sounded a bit sad and discouraged, but as soon as she heard her adult students coming up the steps, she put on her confident, happy smile. "Welcome, welcome," she said. "What in the world is that?"

Tom smiled and handed the red geranium to Dan and

Linda. "It's a present for you both. It's not an ordinary present; it's very special. It's a magic plant."

Hoots, and laughter and quips filled the room: "Tom, I know you're old but I didn't think you were daft!" "Would you like me to bring some fairy dust to sprinkle on it?" "Believe that and I got a bridge to sell you!" and other like-type remarks were made.

Tom laughed along with them, and then told everyone to be very, very quiet. He spoke very quietly and dramatically stretched his arms out in front of him. "Now you've had your fun. Once I was one of 'you' but now I know better. I'm a believer. This *is* a plant that changes people's lives. Something nice happens in the life of the owner. It happened in my life and it changed the life of the person who gave it to me. So, Linda and Dan, I give it to you with my best wishes."

Dan and Linda smiled as they accepted the plant. "Thank you for this beautiful plant and also the thoughts behind it."

"If that's true then I want it next," someone said.

The dance class went well.

"I think the red geranium is working its magic already," Dan said to Linda as they were closing the studio. "For the first time, tonight everyone was laughing and having a good time."

"I noticed that. I also noticed that Tom is becoming a very smooth dancer," Linda told him. "Well, I'm glad everyone had a good time. Maybe it will attract a few new students for us."

Dan nodded his head in agreement. Linda knew he was worried, and so was she.

"Well, we might as well go home and get it over with," he told her.

"I guess so."

"You know, I couldn't get through this without you," Dan said.

"And I definitely couldn't do it without you," she told him as she turned out the lights and they made their way to their car.

In order to preserve their sanity and not worry every minute about money, they had set aside one night a week to discuss finances. They tried to limit all discussion and thoughts of it to that one night. It was always a trying time.

The two had met when they were young dancers just out of school and trying out for a part in a Broadway show. Neither had any money; they existed from one day to the next. When they both had been selected to be in the chorus line of a Broadway show, they felt their dreams had come true. Good things followed for them. Linda was often selected for a solo ballet performance and Dan was selected to be an understudy for the second male star role in a Broadway play. The show ran on Broadway for more than two years. They got married and the world was bright. Since they could list some successes on their resumes, it made parts in other productions easier to obtain. They stayed employed. The positive newspaper reviews of their performances helped launch their careers.

They traveled for two years with a touring company,

doing more and more solo roles. Often they were called on to perform as a couple for private performances. They both felt as if they had wings on their feet. Life was good until…

One day as they were walking across the street in New York, a speeding car fleeing from the police hit both of them. Dan was thrown onto the sidewalk but Linda was crushed by the car. Weeks of hospitalization and therapy followed for both of them. Dan made a full recovery but it took time. It meant he had to start over physically as a dancer. Linda's treatments took another year. She would never again be able to perform the agile movements required by ballet, but able to walk and do most other dances. They had a mountain of bills and no steady income. Their whole world had been dance. They saw no other way to earn a living. They had no way to pay the rent in New York where most of the opportunities for their careers were located.

Dan's grandparents had died and left Dan the small family farm and the remains of their investments. Their home was in a small community outside of Philadelphia. They decided to move to the farm and open a dance studio to teach dancing in the town.

They had a sinking feeling when they saw the farmhouse. It didn't look like the proud, huge, perfect farmhouse Dan remembered from his youth. No upkeep or maintenance had been done on the house for years. But it belonged to them. They made the kitchen, living room and bedroom of the old house livable. The rest of the repairs would have to wait.

While the community was not very large there did

seem to be lots of children in the town. They looked for a space large enough to create a dance studio. They found it on the second floor of an office building. They took enough money from the little they had saved and bought big mirrors for the walls, had a ballet barre installed and invested in a sound system. They decided they should first try to attract the children to teach them various types of dance. They had fliers printed announcing the grand opening and placed them in laundromats and playgrounds. In addition to all types of dance, they included baton lessons.

They attracted many students. The administration at the high school approached them about coaching a dance/drill team to march in front of the band as well as a dance routine for performances. Linda was asked to coach and teach the cheer-leaders. They got no pay for these things, but they hoped the exposure would attract more students for them.

Along with their success came new problems. Many mothers and fathers definitely wanted their children in classes but payments were sporadic. In order to perform, the children needed costumes. Linda decided on red shorts and white T-shirts for them to wear when they marched in the local parades. She shopped in used clothing stores and old costume houses in New York to try to locate costumes she could then sell to the parents at cost for special performances.

Most of the time the outgo of money was greater than their income. They knew something needed to be done. They decided to offer ballroom dancing lessons for adults in the evening. This brought them a little more income. But the people had few places to go to where they could enjoy their new skills. Dan and Linda decided they would offer the space for one dance a week or maybe every two weeks. Music and soft drinks would be furnished. The liquor license to serve wine was too expensive for them to buy at this time. They also charged a fee for dance time. It did help cover the expenses. It also took more of their time to keep the place clean and set-up, and required another supply of music geared for general dancing instead of the strict routine music used for lessons. But the sessions did bring a few new clients for lessons and helped their publicity.

Still, things were very tough for them financially. The hot water heater in their old farm house had stopped working, so they had to get a new one. They weren't sure their furnace would last another winter. The repair man insisted it needed replaced. The windows of the house needed replaced. They were not looking forward to winter. The old house had very little insulation.

They had put off talking about the latest expenses until their weekly financial meeting on Wednesday night.

When they got home from the studio that night, they placed the red geranium on the kitchen table. "Start working your magic, Little Red," Dan said with a smile.

They changed from their dance clothes to their sweats. Linda made coffee and Dan brought all the mail for the week and their bookkeeping ledgers and check books to the kitchen table. They began the grim chore of sorting the mail. Any mail that might have been pleasant had already been opened the day the mail had been delivered. After they had tossed the junk mail they were left with the bills.

Now it was time to move funds between the business and personal check books. There had not been many weeks when the funds moved from business to personal. Usually it was the other way. The amount in their emergency fund kept getting smaller.

"Linda, let's be realistic. How much longer do you think we can hang in here?"

"Not very long," she answered somberly. They sat quietly for a few minutes. "Do you think it is time for us to move back to the city? I know you can find work in the theatre and maybe I can find a job teaching or something," she said.

"I don't know what I'd do in the theatre. Maybe I could get something behind the scenes."

"You're such a great dancer. You're still young enough to understudy again until they recognize your talents," Linda told him.

They sat there, neither saying anything. Then the phone rang.

"Who could be calling so late?" Dan asked as he picked up his phone.

"Dan, old buddy, how are you? I forgot that you farmers might be in bed this early. Hope I didn't wake you up."

"Hello, John," Dan answered. "I was just about to blow out the candles. It gets dark out here in the country mighty early. How are you? How's show business?" He turned to Linda to tell her the caller was John Lupino. "What can I do for you?"

"What you can do is be in the Poconos tomorrow noon for rehearsal at two o'clock."

"What are you talking about?"

"I'm talking about 'Singing in the Rain,' that's what I'm talking about."

"Make sense, John. Remember us farm boys don't talk Broadway."

"I need you to be here to take over the leading role in our play tomorrow night and for the remainder of the show's run here in the Poconos."

"What happened?"

"Our so-call star had a temper tantrum and left the show just before opening tonight. The understudy was so bad I refunded the people's money. You know and have performed that part so many times I know you can step in and do it."

"How long do you need me?"

"The summer theatre will end in two weeks. If sales continue strong like they have been, we may stay another couple of weeks. Can you help us out?"

"Let me talk with Linda. We've got a business going strong here. It's taking both of us to keep up with things."

"Linda is strong, she can do it. This might be a big chance for you. We may take the whole company on tour down through the south. The job could last well into spring."

"I don't want to be away from Linda that long."

"Then bring her along. Is she able to do routines now? We'll put her in the chorus line. I really need you. You know the part so well. I'll tell you what I'll do. I'll double your usual salary."

"I'll call you back in half an hour."

Dan ended the call and sat quietly for a minute or so.

"Tell me about the call," Linda said softly.

He told her what John had said.

Linda listened carefully and then said, "Call him back and tell him you'll be there. I'll start packing for you."

"Linda, I can't. I can't leave you with this financial mess, the dance studio, all of our obligations. Most of all I can't leave you," he said as he moved his chair closer to her and put his arms around her.

"It's not forever, Dan. And the Poconos are not that far. The money you earn will help us with our financial worries. But most importantly, and I truly mean this, Dan, you are a performer. Not every dancer can make a scene come alive. You can. And you and I both know how much you loved it. You gave it all up to stay with me. I love you so much for doing that, but I'm okay now. We don't have to make any long-term plans tonight. Let's look at it as a temporary move. You can be doing something you love and earning money for it. That will pay for a new furnace. I'll stay behind for now and keep up with things here. I'll really miss you but we can still see each other at least once a week."

"I love you, Linda," he said quietly. "There must be some other way."

Linda spoke gently as she handed him his phone. "Just do it."

She kissed him on the top of his head and left the room to start packing his clothes.

As Dan talked with John, his eyes fell on the red

geranium on the kitchen table. *Could it really be magic?* he wondered.

When he got in the car for the drive to the Poconos he still felt guilty about leaving Linda behind. They had always done things together. But they couldn't leave the studio without making some notification to the people. He had to be at the theatre immediately. There was no time for notifying anyone. Anyhow, this job might not last more than two weeks. He knew Linda was strong. Everyone was surprised that not only had she survived the terrible accident but she now had very few limitations on what she could do. As he drove through the quiet dark of the night his worries eventually shifted to what he was doing. He was going back to something he had hoped to do all his life. He was going to dance again. He began to feel as if a burden was being lifted from him. He loved the role he would play. And he knew the role well enough that even if there had been changes made to the scrip for this performance, he could find his way. He could perform this role blind-folded. He began to sing the songs from the musical as his mind recalled the steps to each of them. He pushed the pedal just a little harder to get there a little sooner. *It may not be Broadway but I'm back,* he thought with a smile.

Linda had watched the car drive out of sight. She knew how excited he was to be going back to something he loved. He had given it all up for her. He had not wanted her to give up on a good life. But, New York was a very expensive place for two people to live on a non-star's salary. They had given this move to Pennsylvania a good try, but unless a miracle happened, at least one or maybe both of them would have to try to earn an income some other way. And there weren't too many ways in the area of dance to make it happen. They had already looked into selling the farm, but the housing market experts had advised them to wait at least a year for the market to improve.

Back at the farm, Linda thought about the teaching she was now doing. She did enjoy it. She remembered what one of her ballet teachers had told her. "You do the daily grind of teaching each day, feeling it more and more dull and routine. And then a child appears who has real talent. It makes the whole process of teaching fade into the background as you see that child prosper and grow. It's like watching the flower go from a bud and then reach full bloom." Linda knew she had been the flower for that teacher, Mrs. Bellini.

Mrs. Bellini had been strict and demanding, but when Linda would master a particularly difficult step or routine, Mrs. B. was full of praise and encouragement. It was Mrs. B. who had visited Linda in the hospital at least once a week and never let Linda forget that she could dance again. It was true that Linda could not do all the routines she had done before, but she was able to live a normal life.

As she lay in bed thinking about what might lie ahead for her and Dan, her thoughts drifted to tomorrow's class. It would be a Mother and Toddler dance routine day. Dan had helped her choreograph a program that was fun and charming. She was thinking about asking the moms and kids to perform for the ballroom club. All too soon the hours passed and she was once again on her way to the studio.

On Friday night when the adult dance club met, Linda told them about Dan's return to show business. They were all impressed but worried that the dancing program might end. That night they all took part in helping to clean up and most of them offered to help her if she needed them.

"You are all such really nice people," she told them. "I'm glad you are my friends."

Clair spoke up. "Well, you know why this happened, don't you? It's the magic of the red geranium." The others didn't laugh this time as they looked around skeptically at each other, but no one dared to challenge her.

Each late afternoon Linda and Dan would talk on the phone about their day. Dan sounded very happy to be back in show biz. He constantly told Linda how much he missed her. When Linda found the show would be extended for two more weeks, she made plans to drive to the Poconos to see Dan and the show on a Sunday night.

Linda knew many of the cast members and was greeted warmly. They urged her to come and be part of their company. As she watched the chorus line, she realized that she could do most of the routines they performed. *Should she go back to the theatre*, she wondered? *It would mean looking for a new job as soon as the current show ended. It would mean trying to find an apartment in the city so they had somewhat of a permanent home. It would probably mean living out of suitcases most of the time.* She looked at Dan as he performed on the stage. *He looks so happy*, she thought.

The next morning she took Dan's first paycheck to deposit in the bank. For the first time in many weeks she had money left over to save toward a furnace. As she drove home from the bank she thought about how nice it was when someone on the street would greet her by name and asked her how the dance classes were going. In spite of all the drawbacks and financial worries, she enjoyed having a real home of her own. She had a front porch where she could sit and relax and a kitchen with windows looking out on a beautiful meadow filled with seasonal flowers. She did not have to use elevators to go outside to get fresh air. She did not have to fight traffic in a taxi to get to the grocery store. At the farm she knew the names of her neighbors and they called her by name. Even the cashier at the grocery store called her by her name.

When she got out of the car at the farm, instead of going inside immediately she walked around the property. The sun was shining brightly this morning, making the colors of the falling leaves become vivid and bright. *What a beautiful sight. How amazing it is that each type of tree has leaves that turn a different color. And there are so many different shapes of leaves.* She began to pick up a leaf here and there until her hands were full. She thought about growing up in the city. Walks among the trees were limited to those trees planted in the parks along cement walkways. It was so beautiful and restful to just walk and absorb in all this beauty. Could she ever be content to live in the city again? Could she ever live on the road with all her worldly possessions in a suitcase? She wished she could pick up and box the emotions she was feeling at that moment. She knew that if they sold the farm she might never have a moment like this again. She slowly made her way back to the house. *Back to the routine,* she thought, *but at least I'll have these precious moments to remember.*

Her young students adored her and gave their very best each time they learned something new. She thought about Mrs. B. and discovering a 'blooming flower student.' Linda thought that maybe she had such a student in Anna Marie. Anna Marie was just nine years old but took to ballet with an enthusiasm and talent that was hard to match. Linda and Dan both vowed to work with Anna Marie as much as they could to develop her talent. If the dancing classes ended, it was probable Anna Marie's lessons would also end.

Dan was being pressured to stay with the company and tour through the south when the show in the Poconos ended. One minute Linda was ready to pack up and move to the open road with Dan; the next minute she would think about the studio, the settled living style, and the many friends she had made and decide she didn't want to live on the road. Then the financial picture entered her mind. She really didn't know what to do.

A couple of days later her cell phone rang while she was at the studio waiting for her baton students to arrive.

"Dear sweet Linda, it is so wonderful to finally hear your voice again."

"Mrs. Bellini? Is it really you?"

"Yes, my dear. I have just heard the news that you may be returning to the stage. Is it true? Are you returning to Broadway? Is your body ready to take on that challenge?"

Linda was thrilled to hear her mentor's voice on the phone. "Mrs. B., I can't tell you how happy I am to hear from you. My health is good. How are you and where are you?"

After a few minutes of pleasantries, Mrs. B. said, "Well, enough small talk about the past. Even though I'm glad for all the small talk, tell me more details about you, about your health, about your dance studio, and your plans for the future."

"Mrs. B., are you sure you want to hear all my tales of woe?"

Mrs. B. was quiet for a few seconds and then said quietly, "Tell me everything."

And Linda did tell her everything, the good things and the bad and the uncertainty about the future.

"Thanks for letting me unload on you, Mrs. B. I guess I needed to talk to someone who I know will understand how unsettled I feel about everything. I love Dan and want to be with him and I know he loves me enough to give up his dreams. But I'm beginning to enjoy a more settled kind of living. It would be nice to have a steady income. I don't know if I can have it here. I don't want to be rich, but I don't want to worry about paying the bills. I don't want Dan to give up his dream for me and I don't want to live my life without him here."

"My dear, sweet Linda, you have many decisions to make. I'm afraid my call may make those decisions even harder. I am calling today with a purpose. When I left New York I accepted the position of Dance Master at a prestigious School for the Arts in Pittsburgh. My job was to oversee all the dance classes and their instructors, as well as their teaching style and methods. I love it here. The school accepts talented students of instrumental and vocal music as well as all types of creative art courses, painting and design. I have loved my job as Master of all the dance classes. But I have been promoted to Headmistress of the school. I am looking for someone to fill my shoes as Dance Master. When I asked around the show biz world about you and Dan I had no trouble finding you. You are still remembered for your graceful flying leaps on the stage. My purpose in calling you was to offer you the position of Dance Master. I did not know Dan had returned to the stage or that you might join him there." She paused thoughtfully.

"Mrs. B., are you serious? You would really consider me for this position? I am so thrilled. I know I could never fill your shoes but I am so honored that you would think of me. My initial reaction is to say that I will be there tomorrow. It's a position I think I would love. But I could only do it with Dan by my side. He seems to be enjoy being back on the stage. And I don't want to be separated from him for long periods of time. I don't know what to tell you."

"Linda, dear, I know this takes you by surprise. I wish I had a position to offer Dan at the school, but our staff is set for the year. Pittsburgh does have an active theatre group here. There are several really good playhouses in the area and their summer music theatre program is one of the best in the states. There are some opportunities for

Dan here. But I know that sometimes nothing can replace Broadway."

She paused, then continued, "I'm sorry if I'm adding to the pressure you have right now, but there is one more thing. I need someone immediately. I've been trying to do both my old and new job for a few weeks and I can't do it any longer. I need help now. You would not need to worry about a place to live here. One of our benefactors purchased a four-unit condominium building so that when we have guest teachers or performers come to town they can stay right near campus. You could use one of those units for one year, rent free. The trustees know how desperate I am so they are freshening up the unit with new paint, etc. It's a two bedroom unit so you could use one room as an office."

"It sounds like a wonderful, wonderful opportunity but I must talk with Dan. Can I call you back tomorrow?"

"Of course. I'm sorry I can't give you more time."

"You're being very generous. I'll call you tomorrow."

As Linda ended the call she thought about the red geranium at home on the kitchen table.

"Little Red, I don't understand what you're doing, but I love you. Even if Dan wants to make other plans, my morale has been boosted to the heavens. Thank you, Little Red."

The class for the baton lessons had arrived while Linda was on the phone. Linda wasn't sure if the students were especially gifted that day or if it was her mood, but teaching the class was fun and rewarding. When each baton was thrown into the air it was caught by person who threw it. That was a first for this class.

As soon as class was over, she decided to leave Dan a message to call her. She knew he might be on his way for the evening performance at the theatre.

Before she had a chance to dial his number her cell phone rang. It was Dan.

"Hi, Babe," he said cheerfully. "I got big news. We are closing the show tonight. And as soon as I can I'll be on the road to come home. Isn't 'home' a nice word?"

"Dan, I didn't expect you for at least another week. I'll be so glad to have you here!"

"Well, I'm at the theatre now. We're going to start packing up what we can so everyone can get out a little earlier. I'll talk to you later. Love you."

Linda was elated. Now she could tell him in person about the offer from Mrs. Bellini. Then she got a bit concerned. *Maybe Dan will just be home for a day or so and then on the road again. Or maybe he has decided he wants to go back to the city and try to find work on Broadway. Well, if that's what he wants, I'll be by his side. Maybe I won't even tell him about the offer I have received.* She began to count down the hours until he would be home.

Dan got home around three that morning. Since they had no classes to teach the next day, and they didn't go to bed until after four a.m., they slept late. After a big breakfast, almost in unison they said, "We need to talk."

"Linda, do you want to go first or shall I?"

"Why don't you talk first?" Linda answered for she had made up her mind not to tell him about the offer if he wanted to return to New York. She wanted to be with him. She wanted them both to be happy.

"When I left for the Poconos I was so excited to be going back on the stage I sang all the way there that first night. The old excitement of the audience and applause filled me with joy. I only needed you there to make it perfect. But it only took two nights for that old feeling to disappear. I began to hear the bickering among the cast. I guess when I had you near me I didn't hear it. Everyone was worried about how long the show would run and what they would do next. I had forgotten that side of the business. I realized I really missed going to our studio. I missed the kids and even the members of our dance club. I missed the routine we have been able to develop here in spite of our money worries. I missed the friends we have made. I guess I even missed this old drafty farmhouse.

"I don't want us to be separated again. If you want to return to New York and performing, I'll be with you one hundred percent. But if you want to stay here and keep trying to make a go of it, I'll be with you one hundred percent for that choice, too. I think that in time we can make a go of this business. But I think I should look for another job somewhere here in town to help us out financially for a while. We both don't really need to be at the studio all the time. You have managed so well without me. And I can take over the studio so that you can get a break from it."

"Oh, Dan, are you really, really sure you feel that way?"

"Yes, it's how I feel. Yet I'll be fine if you want to go back to New York."

She reached out to take his hand. "I had a phone call yesterday from Mrs. Bellini."

"Does she have a dancing job for you? If she does, you must give it a try."

"It was about a job, but it's not the kind you are thinking about."

Linda took time to tell him about the offer Mrs. B. had made. He listened quietly and thoughtfully.

"Did you tell her you'd be there this week?"

"Of course not, you silly goose. We need to think about this."

"If you are hesitating because you are thinking about my career you must not do that. As a matter of fact, I started thinking again about directing, like I'd done in college. I loved doing it. I even thought of small ways I would change a couple of routines we were performing in 'Dancing' to make them fresh and new. It is so different from performing, yet still offers the best of both worlds. Pittsburgh has lots of opportunities connected to the theatre. This could be a brand new start for us. Since we won't have to pay rent for a place to live, we should have no money worries while we're getting settled. As for you, don't be modest now. You know this is a perfect job for you."

"It does sound pretty special," Linda said quietly.

"Call Mrs. B. and tell her you'll be there right away."

"I think we should think it over for a couple of days."

"Babe, what did you tell me when John Lupino called me to come right away?"

"That was different."

"No, it was not different. You sent me on my way. Knowing I was going with your blessing made it easier for me. Now I want to make it easy for you. Here's your phone. Call her."

"Dan, the studio, the classes…."

"You managed them fine without me here. Now I can take a turn managing them. Linda, our lease on the studio will run out at the end of the year. That will give me time to find a buyer or close the studio. Pittsburgh is not that far. We can still see each other often. I am confident I will find work in Pittsburgh." He paused as a new thought entered his mind. "Do you think we should try to sell the farm right away? Even if the real estate market is lower right now…"

Linda interrupted. "In spite of its run-down condition I'm beginning to love the place. It is so restful here. Could we try to hold on to it for a least a while?"

"Maybe we could do that," he said with a smile. "I understand the house has a beautiful red geranium blooming in the kitchen."

By the end of the week Linda was on her way to Pittsburgh with the red geranium in the back seat. Dan had insisted she take it with her. He told her he knew Little Red would take care of her. Their condo would not be ready for two more weeks, but Mrs. B. had found an apartment about seven miles from the school where she could live temporarily. As Linda drove along the Pennsylvania Turnpike to get to Pittsburgh she felt a sense of peace come over her. She was not so naïve that she expected everything would be perfect, but she felt that now she had a path for her life. With Dan by her side, she knew they would be fine.

The next two weeks passed quickly for both Dan and Linda. She had been warmly received by the other staff members at the school. The staff she would supervise all seemed competent and the children seemed talented and respectful. In her quieter moments, Linda felt as if she had her dream job.

Back at the dance studio Dan prepared some notices that they would be closing. The parents of the young children were sad and dismayed with the news. But the dance club members were stunned when they heard about it.

"Now we know enough to have fun dancing. Where will we go? Who will teach us the new steps? What can we do about this?" they asked Dan.

"Well, maybe you can look for a buyer for the business. It's a good little business but needs someone here full time. I don't want to be separated from Linda so I can't stay. But I'd be willing to sell it if I could find a buyer," he told the members.

"No one could replace you and Linda," they told him. "We will really miss you."

"We're going to hold on to the farm, so we'll be back quite often," Dan said, "and I hope to see each of you when we do come back."

Clair and Tom had sat without speaking while Dan talked with the members of their group. Suddenly, Clair stood up. "Dan, if I were to buy this business, what would I need to make it a success?"

"Probably a good instructor and patience to listen to that person gripe," Dan answered.

"Tom, could you manage the business end?" Clair asked as she turned to him.

"What's one more business to manage to me?" he answered with a wave of his hand.

"If we can find a good instructor, I'll buy the business," Clair said.

"I like the idea of having a local owner," one of the men said. "Maybe I'd like to buy some shares in the business. My wife and I are really enjoying the class as well as our dance night."

Another woman said, "I think we all should be given the opportunity to buy a share." The members began to talk among themselves.

Dan asked for their attention. "Why don't I do this? I will try to locate an instructor you can hire. You can meet privately and decide if one or maybe more than one person wants in on the sale of the business. Talk with your business managers. I will have my books open for your representative to look at. Shall we postpone any more discussion until next week?"

They agreed on Dan's plan. Dan was so excited by the discussion. As soon as the crowd left he pulled out his phone to call Linda. It was nearly midnight but he knew she would not mind being awakened by this news.

Linda was thrilled and excited when she heard about

the possible sale of the studio. "Do you have anyone special in mind to be the instructor?" she asked him.

"I'm thinking about JoAnn and Bob. They've been talking about retiring for a few years now. They both made good money performing and I know he invested wisely. But I'm not sure they'd be interested for I heard him say something about working on a cruise ship just to stay in touch with dancing."

"They would be perfect. Why don't you give them a call and give them some time to consider it."

"Okay, then I'll do it." Dan paused and then said, "Linda, can you really believe how our lives are finally coming together. It doesn't seem possible."

"It's like a miracle." Linda said. "But I have some news for you. The condo is now ready for us. I'm going to move in this weekend. I've been giving a lot of thought to Little Red. We have already had so many good things happen I wonder if I should pass it on. What do you think?"

"I think I'd like to keep it forever," he said with a laugh. "I'm a grown man standing here talking about a magic plant. Can you believe it?"

"Maybe I should leave it here in the apartment for the next tenant. Yes, I think that is what I will do."

The next day as Linda went to leave the apartment for the last time, there was a knock on the door followed by a voice saying "Housekeeping. It's Theresa Simpson."

Linda opened the door and told the woman she could come in, then, made her way to the elevator. Suddenly she heard a voice calling to her to wait. "You forgot your plant, ma'am."

"Theresa, I decided to leave it for the next tenant. It's a very special plant. I think the new tenant will enjoy it."

Linda made her way to her car to drive to her new home and officially begin her new life. She was very happy.

That night Linda received a phone call from Theresa, who was crying.

"Ma'am, I have some very bad news for you. After you left and I was cleaning so the new tenant can move in, I accidentally knocked the plant off the counter. It broke one of the sides off the plant. My sister is visiting me and we called every florist in Pittsburgh but no one has a blooming geranium so I can replace it. I'm so sorry." She began to weep again.

"Theresa, don't cry. It's okay."

"You don't understand. If you report me to the manager I'll lose my job."

"Theresa, I know it was an accident. You have been very good to me these last couple of weeks. I will not report you to management."

"Really?"

"Really."

"Well, ma'am, I'm not giving up. My sister told me there is a plant doctor in the town where she lives. She's going to take the remains of this plant to him. Maybe he'll be able to save the plant. I will make sure that it is returned to the apartment. Thank you so much for understanding."

"It was a very special plant. But even special plants come to the end of their days. Please don't worry about it, Theresa. Thank you for telling me about the accident. And please don't worry, it can be our secret."

CHAPTER 9
BRYAN

Bryan pulled into the driveway, got out of his van and walked to the street. He really did walk to the street but he felt as if he was floating down the driveway. He could not believe how he had turned his life around in one year. He looked around at his new property. It was *HIS* property. Last year he had been living on the streets. Now, he was the owner of a business. Oh, how he wished his grandmother could see him now! He looked at the front of his shop, designed to look like a house with a red roof. Above the entry was a sign:

THE RED GERANIUM

Plant Doctor
Fresh Flowers
Plant Rental

At the bottom of the sign was a picture of a full, blooming red geranium. *This is mine*, he thought, *this is mine*. He opened the door, stepped inside and looked around the shop.

"I can tell you did it, Bryan," Emily Roberts said as he stepped inside the shop. Emily worked as an office/sales rep and had been with the shop for more than ten years. "With that grin on your face I know that everything went well and you are now the owner."

"You are so right, Emily. The shop is now mine!" He waved a handful of papers in the air. "All these papers say it's mine."

"Well, congratulations, Bryan. I know you'll make a success of the business here. You'll be pleased to know that we had two more calls come in for plant rentals while you were gone. I asked for some tentative ideas about the types of plants they were looking for and said you would call them back."

"What would I do without you, Emily?" he said with a smile as he reached over and gave her a hug. "You have been so supportive. I really owe you a great big thank you. Are you and Paul free to join me for dinner? You really helped make all this possible."

"Thanks for the invitation but there's a football game tonight at the high school and we want to be there to support young Paul. I should leave right now unless you have something more for me to do today. You need to go and have a great night out in our big city of Zanesville and be ready for a busy day tomorrow."

"Go home and enjoy yourself. I'll take you and Paul out another time. Were there any other calls?"

"Just one. Someone wanted to know if we carry geraniums. I explained they were a spring and summer plant in our climate. The woman insisted she had to have one so I told her you would call."

After Emily left, Bryan looked with happiness around his shop. *I did it, Grandma, I did it.*

Meyer Higgs had owned Bryan's plant rental and flower business, placing fresh flowers on consignment in various grocery stores, including Pete's Grocery Store. When Mr. Higgs had first approached Bryan about buying his business, Bryan was trying to prove to himself that he could be stable and make a new life for himself. Bryan had told Mr. Higgs a little about his past and how he needed six months to prove to himself that he had really left the past behind. Mr. Higgs had been very understanding and said he was willing to wait the time, but he needed someone right away to manage the business. He asked Bryan to work for him and said if it worked out well for both of them, he would wait to sell the shop until Bryan was ready.

Bryan knew that Mr. Higgs could no longer keep up his business because his health was declining. His place of business was about seven miles outside Zanesville, and at one time had been very successful. He had taken Bryan to see the place. The property was situated on two acres. There was a building in front which housed a small shop, a big workroom in the back and an apartment on the second floor. Behind the building was a greenhouse of medium size. Mr. Higgs housed the plants in the greenhouse that he rented out to businesses. After being in a restaurant or business office for some time, the plants often would look weak and anemic. Mr. Higgs would replace the rental plants with healthy ones and bring the old ones back for some TLC. As a side line to increase income, Mr. Higgs started the grocery store floral consignments. He told Bryan how much his late wife had loved the business. But now she was gone. His daughter wanted him to move out of state to live near her.

Bryan told Mr. Higgs about his dream to either work with or teach about plants. Someday he hoped to have his own landscaping business. Bryan had many ideas for reaching a sales goal. One was to plant seeds for garden flowers in the greenhouse to be ready to be sold as small plants in the spring. He felt that it could start him on to even more and bigger things, perhaps someday even into the landscaping business.

Bryan had begun to allow himself to dream big for his future. After receiving Mr. Higgs' permission to give him an answer after the first of the year, Bryan left Pete's Grocery and went to work with Mr. Higgs. Bryan loved his work; Mr. Higgs loved Bryan's enthusiasm for the place. Bryan had the money from the sale of his grandmother's house transferred from Maine to Zanesville and then secured a loan for the balance of what he thought he needed to be successful.

And now, as Bryan stood looking around the shop, he began to smile again. He did a little dance and said, "It's mine! It's mine!"

He decided to close the shop early so he locked the

door and went upstairs to his apartment. He had moved into the apartment when he took over the management of the shop. Bryan stood and shook his head when he thought about all the changes in his life in the past year. He felt very fortunate to have turned his life around. One of his proudest moments had been when he went to the VA hospital for his annual check-up. The doctors there pronounced him well and healthy. Of course he then lost his VA disability pension. But he felt so proud that he had left the demons of his disability behind.

"I guess it was all because of a red geranium," he said aloud. He normally did not believe in nonsense like magic, but he did have to admit swapping it for a meal with Pete and Jeannie had changed his life. He realized that not only did he have his health, he had a business, and now he had a family. Pete and Jeannie were always there for him, encouraging and supporting him.

The next morning he was up early and went to the greenhouse where he checked his "ailing" plants. He was satisfied that most were ready to go back to some store or restaurant.

He walked to the window and looked out at the woods behind his building which today were covered with snow. The bare branches of some of the trees were dancing in the wind in a striking contrast to the deep green of the evergreen trees in their midst. Bryan walked to another window to look over the Christmas trees he had brought on consignment to sell. He had a selection of cut trees but also some that were live and potted in tubs. He had some Christmas roping and wreaths. *Next year,* he thought; *next year, I will purchase the trees and skip the middleman so I can earn more profit.*

He took time to check out his plans for starting flower garden plants in the spring. He wondered if he should plant some tomato and pepper plants in addition to the flowers. He had been approached by a dealer in garden supplies who wanted Bryan to carry their products. The front office would not have space for them. These were not things that worried him, but enjoyable evidence that he now owned his business.

He heard the phone ring.

"Hello, this is Calvin Webster. I own the Webster Resort over in Fairview. Perhaps you've heard of us?"

"Yes, indeed, Mr. Webster. What can I do for you?"

"I hear you are a plant doctor. Is that so?"

"I like healthy plants. I do my best to keep them that way."

"Do you have other clients on our side of the mountain?"

"Not at the present time, but you're not far away. Do you have some ailing plants?"

"I just noticed this morning that the various plants I have in the lobby and banquet room are looking really bad. We are having a major banquet here tonight. I was wondering if you have any healthy plants we might be able to rent right away."

After a brief discussion, Bryan knew he had enough plants on hand to fill the request. These were plants he planned to exchange in the next couple of weeks in various restaurants around town. But he knew of a good resource in Pittsburgh where he could buy additional replacements. This might be an opportunity for him to expand his business in a new area. He told Mr. Webster he would be there in an hour or so.

His business was not usually open on Saturday this late in the fall, so when he heard someone pounding on his door, he was surprised. He opened the door and found a woman standing there holding a red geranium in her hands. It did not appear to be in very good shape. Part of it had been broken off and pushed into the soil.

"Come in," he said. "It's unusual to see a red geranium this time of year. How can I help you?"

"I'm Mrs. Harrington. I left a message for you but you didn't call me back," she said.

"I'm sorry. I intended to call you later today. Are you the lady who called wanting to buy a geranium?"

"Yes, I did. And it's critical that I find one."

"A blooming geranium may be difficult to locate this time of year. But I see you have one already."

"My sister broke this one. She may lose her job if we don't find a replacement right away."

Bryan took the plant from Mrs. Harrington, and began to look at it with a critical eye. "Tell me what happened."

"My sister is a cleaning lady at an apartment complex in Pittsburgh. A lady was moving out of an apartment. She left without the plant. My sister ran after her with the plant but the woman said it was for the next person who moved into the apartment. I guess the tenants must have known each other. While my sister was cleaning she accidentally knocked it off the kitchen counter. As you can see she broke the plant. My sister's boss is very particular about any damage that might occur and makes the employee pay for it. Sometimes the employee gets fired. She tried to find a replacement for it but couldn't find one. She called me. I called you but you weren't here. I love my sister and I know she really, really needs her job. Your sign says you are a plant doctor. So I brought the plant back from Pittsburgh last night. Can you fix it right away so I can take it back to her?"

Bryan really wanted to help her. But Bryan also wanted to get the plants in his van to the resort on the other side of the mountain. It could mean more business for him. Still, he did have a special spot in his heart for red geraniums even if this plant may have been damaged beyond repair.

"May I confirm your telephone number? The plant is damaged, but I think I can fix it. If not, I'll try my best to find a replacement. I'll call you later, maybe this afternoon. How does that sound?"

As Mrs. Harrington left the shop with a sad face, she turned to Bryan and said. "You must think I'm crazy fussing about this, but my sister is just finding her way back in the world after a very long illness. If she were to lose her job…"

Bryan felt great sympathy. "Sometimes red geraniums have a magic all their own. I may be able to save it. I promise you, I will call you this afternoon."

As Bryan drove over the mountains with the potted plants in the back of his van, he started to grin. *Oh, the joys of being a business owner*, he thought.

The plants at the resort were in a bad condition. Mr.

Webster was very happy when the plants Bryan brought were carefully placed in locations not only attractive but also good for them. The resort's original plants were placed in the back of Bryan's van for a little rest and relaxation and tender loving care. Bryan told Mr. Webster he would be back in a couple of weeks to check on the plants.

"Bring a contract with you," Mr. Webster told him. "I will appreciate having someone look after the plants."

As Bryan drove back home he thought about the red geranium. He would always have a special spot in his heart for red geraniums. Last spring when Jeannie opened her renovated hair salon, Bryan had given her a red geranium which she placed on the front desk. Maybe Jeannie would be willing to give it up to save a woman's job. Still, he mused, it might be possible to fix the original so that no one would ever know it was broken.

It was late afternoon by the time Bryan had a chance to look at the geranium. The break of the stock had been a crooked one and already some of the leaves had started to turn brown and curl up. He could see the soil was tight on the plant and knew it probably had been some time since it had been repotted. He carried the plant to his potting table and began carefully to remove it from the pot.

He heard the bell in the front office ring, followed by the sound of a key in the lock, and the friendly voice of Jeannie calling out, "It's just us. Should we come to the back room or upstairs?"

"I'm back here and you won't believe what I've got," he called back to her.

"We insist on taking you out to celebrate tonight.

Bryan, we're so proud of you," Jeannie said as she and Pete came into the back room.

"Did everything go okay yesterday when you closed the deal?" Pete asked.

"Things went great. I've already picked up a new customer. The manager of the resort over in Fairview called me early this morning needing some replacement plants for tonight. I just got back a few minutes ago."

"What's that you're working on?" Jeannie asked. "It looks like a red geranium."

"It is indeed." Bryan told them about the visit from the woman that morning. "This is the first time I've had to look at it." He continued to work as he talked. "What in the world is that?" he said aloud.

Pete and Jeannie came close to look.

"Looks like somebody crumbled up some foil and shoved it in the pot."

Being careful not to disturb the roots he carefully pulled the foil away. He laid it on the work table and continued to work on the root system of the plant. Then he picked up the broken branch and looked at it carefully.

"I don't know why I say this, but somehow I feel I can just place this broken branch back in the pot next to the host plant and it will grow," Bryan said.

"Well, it might be worth a try. No one might ever know the difference and the woman won't lose her job," Pete said.

"Is each geranium different from the others?" Jeannie asked.

"Of course, though to most folks they look pretty similar," Bryan answered.

"That plant looks familiar to me," Jeannie said.

They all laughed as they remembered how a red geranium changed their lives.

"Give me ten minutes to repot the plant and call the customer. In honor of the celebration we're having tonight and because geraniums are special to us all, I won't even charge her."

"You're a good man, Bryan."

Bryan dialed the woman's number and while he waited for the call to go through he began to return the tools to the rack and brush off the counter. There was no answer. As he ended the call, he saw the little packet of foil that he had retrieved from the plant. As the three stood there in idle chatter, his fingers began to smooth out the foil.

"This looks like a packet, not just a ball of foil," he said. He carefully pulled back one layer, then another, and stopped and looked up at Jeannie and Pete. "You won't believe this. I think there is a message in this plant."

He removed the last of the foil and found a hand-written note:

"This is a magic plant. It will bring you good luck. Take care of it"

He handed the note to Pete who read it and then passed it to Jeannie.

They all stood silent for a couple of minutes. Then they looked at each other.

"Could it be possible that this is the plant you gave us?" Pete asked.

"I doubt that," Bryan answered. "Didn't it end up going to the Philadelphia area of the state?"

Jeannie went over and touched the plant. "This makes me feel eerie. Somehow I think this is the same plant."

"I'm sure it is," Pete said playfully. "And the little green men from Mars keep moving it around the country."

"You can laugh at me all you want. But, Bryan, that plant you gave us was magic. I think it's the same plant," Jeannie insisted.

"Well, I'm hungry," Bryan said. "Let's go eat. Maybe we can figure out a way to find out if it's the same one."

The discussion over dinner, centered on whether it was even possible this could be the same plant given to Bryan when he lived under the highway. They decided there would never be a way to tell. Or could this possibly be a second magic red geranium? After dessert they went back to Bryan's, walked over to the plant and stood looking at it.

"Do you think we could contact the person who left the plant in the apartment? Maybe we could come up with some excuse for calling," Pete said.

"I might tell her it's a special variety I'm tracking," Bryan said.

"How can you start your search?" Jeannie asked.

"We'll have to start with the woman who owned the plant and was giving it away. I'll call my customer right now."

There was still no answer to his call so he again left his name and phone number on the answering machine.

Late that evening, Bryan got a return call from Mrs. Harrington.

"Please forgive me for calling so late. I'm calling from Pittsburgh. My sister had a major relapse and I'm with her at the hospital. I don't know when I'll be home. Can you keep the plant for me for a few days longer?"

"Of course I can. Do you by any chance know the name of the woman who occupied the apartment and left the plant?"

"No, but I know her name and number are in my sister's apartment. My sister called the tenant and told her about breaking the plant. My sister told the woman she might lose her job and the woman told her not to worry, that accidents happen. She said it would be their secret."

"Sounds like she was a nice person. Did your sister have any information about who she is?"

"Theresa said she is some big-shot teacher who just came to teach at the School for the Arts in Pittsburgh."

"Tell your sister not to worry about the plant. I'm standing here looking at it right now and only an expert could even tell it was broken. I'll take care of it for her."

That night when Bryan lay in bed he thought back to the night he had discovered the geranium. He remembered the days of walking in the rain not having any idea where the road would take him. It took him to recovery. *I hope this plant has recovery powers and that I can return it back to Theresa.*

On Sunday morning he met Pete and Jeannie at church and then went back to their house to watch the Pittsburgh Steelers play football and have a chicken dinner.

"Were you able to reach Mrs. Harrington last night about returning the plant?" Jeannie asked.

Bryan told them about the phone call and Theresa's relapse. Then he continued, "I don't know why I did it, but I did ask about who owned the plant. Mrs. Harrington didn't know the person's name but did say she is a new teacher at the School for the Arts in Pittsburgh."

Pete spoke up. "I bet I can get her name for you. Our former mayor was on the Board of Director's there. I'll give him a call."

He went right to the phone. A few minutes later the call was returned.

Pete was smiling. "Well, he's pretty confident the name of the person we want is Linda Hausman. She was just hired to be the new Dance Master at the school. She and her husband are former dancers. She is now living in a condo just off campus. Here's her number. How about it, Bryan? Are you curious enough to give her a call?"

Jeanne spoke up. "If you're not, I am. Bryan, you've got to call her."

"Oh, why not?" Bryan said. "Everything about that plant has been crazy – crazy good." He picked up the phone.

"Dan Hausman here," a voice came over the line.

"Mr. Hausman, my name is Bryan Winters. I'm calling from Zanesville. Did you and your wife recently transfer to Pittsburgh? Is your wife the new Dance Master at the School for the Arts?"

"We are, indeed. My wife is right here. Do you need to talk with her?"

"If I could, please, I would appreciate it. I won't be long."

"This is Linda, how can I help you?"

"Mrs. Hausman, my name is Bryan Winters. I own a garden and nursery facility in Zanesville. Yesterday, a customer brought in a red geranium plant..."

"Dan, pick up the phone," Linda interrupted. "It's about Little Red."

"What? I'm on the line also. Did something happen to Little Red?"

"Little Red?" Bryan asked.

"You wouldn't believe me if I told you about the plant," Linda began. "I know the plant was dropped. Theresa called to tell me. You're not calling to tell me that Theresa got fired, are you? I promised her I wouldn't say a word."

"My call is about the plant. It's doing well. Theresa's sister brought the plant to me. I was able to repot and repair it for Theresa. When I called about returning it to her I was told that Theresa has had a relapse of an old illness and is very ill in the hospital. Can you tell me who the plant belongs to now? I understand you left it for someone else."

"Actually, I don't know. You may think I'm crazy but there's a story connected to Little Red," she began.

"I doubt I'll think you're crazy, and I'd like to hear your story. I'd like to ask my two friends who are with me to hear the story also. Do you have any objections?"

"I don't really object although if my new bosses hear me tell it they may want me to leave my job."

"It can be our secret," Bryan told her.

"Dan, my husband, and I were dancers on Broadway until we were involved in a car accident. About a year ago we left New York to move to Dan's grandparents' farm in Tarrytown, which had been left to him. We opened a dance studio there. In spite of our love for the house and the people there, having a dance studio in town was challenging. We had some financial set-backs. One night, one of our adult students came to class carrying the red geranium. He said it was a magical good-luck plant that brought nice things to whoever owned it. He said it had helped him and also the person who gave it to him. Then he gave it to us. We took it home and named it Little Red. Almost immediately nice things started to happen. Dan was called to perform in a play in the Poconos. While he was gone, I got a call offering me the position of Dance Master here at the school. Our luck certainly did turn around. We found a buyer for our business. I brought Little Red with me when I moved here. I stayed in an apartment complex while our condo was being painted. When I moved here to the condo I thought I should follow the tradition of passing Little Red along. I had no idea who the person who was moving into the apartment after me, might be. He or she did not know they were receiving it. It makes me sad to think that Theresa has had so much worry about breaking it."

"Did you ever have it re-potted?" Bryan asked.

Dan answered, "No. Actually we only had the plant for a few weeks. We named it Little Red and talked to it. But you do not seem surprised by our story. What's going on?"

"Mr. and Mrs. Hausman, I do not think you are going crazy. Honestly, I think I may have had this magical plant at one time and I'm trying to trace where it's been to see if it is the same plant. I know of at least three other people who had the plant after me. All of us had good fortune come our way. I live in Zanesville which is in the mountain area of western Pennsylvania. Would you mind telling me where Tarrytown is located?"

"It's about thirty miles from Philadelphia," Linda said.

Dan spoke up. "We can give you the name of the man who gave us the plant. He owns Independent Tool and Die Company there. It's Tom Patterson. I have a phone number for him packed away in some of our boxes. Would you like me to dig it out and call you back?"

"That won't be necessary. I can find his company on the internet and call."

"Did good things happen to you when you had the plant?" Linda asked.

"So many good things you wouldn't believe it. I'm sorry I've taken so much of your time, but you have been very, very helpful. Thank you so much."

"If you do trace it back, could you let us know the history of the magical plant?"

"I'll let you know."

As he ended the call, Bryan said, "It's got to be the same plant. Remember when Alma left the plant outside her door and the young couple found it. They lived in the Philadelphia area. It's got to be the same plant. Well, I guess I'll have to track down Tom Patterson. His company is probably closed today. I'll call him first thing in the morning."

When Emily came to work the next morning, Bryan had already been busy with his plants for a couple of hours. She spotted the red geranium on the counter in the office.

"Wow. That plant looks great. Is it the one that a Mrs. Harrington called about?"

"Yes. I'm going to take care of it for a little while."

Emily, who had already heard the story of Bryan's magic red geranium started to laugh. "What is it with you and red geraniums? You must have a magnet on you."

Bryan poured two cups of coffee and offered one to Emily. "You won't believe what Pete and Jeannie made me do," he smiled. He told her about Mrs. Harrington's hospitalized sister and the investigation he, Pete, and Jeannie had begun.

"What's the name of the company where Tom works? I'll get right on it. This is important stuff," Emily said. She made few clicks on her computer and turned to Bryan and said "I'm calling him now."

Bryan stood by listening to her conversation.

"Is Mr. Patterson in this morning? I see. Yes. Yes. Let me make sure I have the name right. It's Rosie's Yarn Shop. Is Rosie spelled with an 'ie' or a 'y'? Okay, then. Thank you so much."

Turning to Bryan, she said, "Tom Patterson is semi-retired from the tool and die company but spends a lot of time at his other business, Rosie's Yarn Shop. I have the number right here."

Seconds later, she said, "This is Mrs. Roberts from the Red Geranium shop in Zanesville, calling for Mr. Patterson. Is he available?" After a moment of listening, she covered the phone and told Bryan, "Mr. Patterson is on a vacation to the West Coast. His store manager, Maureen McDowell is on the line."

"I'll talk with her," Bryan said.

"Mrs. McDowell, my name is Bryan Winters. I am a plant doctor in Zanesville. I had a special red geranium plant brought in for some care. I'm trying to track down its history."

"Mr. Winters, at one time I owned a special magic red geranium. And no, Mr. Winters, I do not believe in fairy dust and goblins. But it was a really special plant."

"Is it special because when you got it you were told good things happen to anyone who owns it?" Bryan asked.

"Mr. Winters, I'm stunned. You are right. How did you know? Where is Zanesville? If it is the same plant, how it get so far from Tarrytown?"

"That's what I'm trying to find out. It's entirely possible that I owned this plant at one time. Good things happened to me and to the next three people who owned it. I'm very curious to know if it is the same plant."

"I'll tell you what I know about it. I had a job working with computer systems that I hated and was no good at. I was terminated. On one of my last days of work one of our management team complimented me about the sweater I was wearing. I told her I had knit it. Knitting is my passion. Anyhow, about a week later this same nice woman came to my house bringing me a red geranium. She said she had been given the plant and it brought many nice things to her and her husband. The plant also worked its magic for me. I got a new job managing Rosie's Yarn Shop. I also knit sweaters for customers. I'm proud to say my sweaters have been selected for an upcoming fashion show in New York.

"There's more magic. Rosie's Yarn Shop was owned by Tom and Rosie Patterson. Rosie died and Tom spent most of his days grieving. He was not interested in the Tool and Die Company he owned and didn't know much about yarns. He was existing, not living. He put a sign in his window for help. I saw his sign when I came to buy yarn. He hired me that day. My life turned around I have been very happy and our business is doing very well. But I could see that Tom was very lonely so I gave him the red geranium with hopes he could find happiness. And he did. An old friend returned to town. She charmed him into changing his life and his life style. Today he is a very happy man. I'm sure that red geranium has magic powers."

"It seems that everyone who has owned the geranium has had something good happen to them. I have two questions for you. Do you know to whom Tom gave the plant and second, who gave you the plant?"

"He gave it to a couple who ran a dance studio here. Dance lessons became one of the ways he changed his life. I know the couple left town and I believe they moved to Pittsburgh."

"They did indeed. And they also have had good things happen to them. Would you mind giving me the name of the person who gave you the plant?"

"It was given to me by Judy Dixon. She and her husband were on a Christmas vacation at a resort in Fairview. They found the plant in the snow at a mountain home they hoped to buy. When they tried to find the owner, a man who owns a grocery store there told them it was a magic plant and the plant now belonged to them. They really loved that plant. It did bring them good fortune. Jeff got a big promotion at work and they now have a baby boy they both adore after many years of trying to have a family."

"Mrs. McDowell, may I call you Maureen? I feel like this plant has made us family. I know now how the plant passed from me to Pete and Jeannie who helped me get back a life after living on the streets for a time. Jeannie and Pete were still suffering the loss of their son in the war in Iraq and feeling sad. They opened their hearts and home to me. While trying to take care of me, they also began to live their lives again.

"On Thanksgiving Day they gave the plant to a sweet little old lady who lived alone on the top of the mountain. She was very isolated and would not reach out to anyone. I was with her when Pete and Jeannie gave the plant to her. Very soon after she started to live her life again which included reconciling with her daughter. She is now very happy. She accidentally left the plant behind when she went to be with the daughter for the Christmas holidays. The plant was left on the driveway. Jeff and Judy were hiking in the mountains and found the plant. They were referred to Pete, who is also the mayor of our town. Alma had already told Pete about leaving the plant behind and said it should be kept by whoever found it. That turned out to be Jeff and Judy. So this little plant has quite a history."

"Do you mind my asking who gave you the plant? Did that person have good luck?" Maureen asked Bryan.

"I don't know. I guess we never will. I was living on the streets. I was sleeping in an underpass on the highway near Pittsburgh when someone left it by my side along with some food. My companions and I ate the food that night. But I couldn't get back to sleep. I picked up the plant and left the shelter of the highway and began to walk. Eventually I made my way to a grocery store about seventy-five miles away. Pete and Jeannie took me in and helped me have a new life. I now have my own business working with plants and flowers and I'm very happy. That plant started me on my new life."

"Well, I'll certainly have to tell Tom about all this when he returns," Maureen told him. "I feel really special to have been a part of...well, I guess we can call it the history of a beautiful plant. But how did it end up with you again?"

"Last Saturday a woman brought it to me. It had been dropped and a branch had broken off. I have the plant here at my greenhouse. I have confirmed that the person who brought the plant to Pittsburgh is Linda Hausman from the dance studio. She brought it with her when she moved from Tarrytown. She didn't know who would be moving into the apartment she used for a couple of weeks. But she felt she and her husband had so many nice things happen that she should leave it for the next tenant. A woman cleaning the apartment accidentally knocked it off a counter. She worked in an apartment complex with very strict rules in place about any damage an employee might cause. The woman was afraid she would lose her job. She became very ill. Her sister lives in Zanesville where I have my business. She brought it to me to see if it could be saved. This little plant has been all over Pennsylvania."

"Are you able to save it?" Maureen asked.

"It looks very good right now. I think it will be fine."

"I'll be sure to tell Tom and also let Judy and Jeff know about your call. I hope that something else really good happens to you before you pass it on again."

Emily had been listening to the conversations. She sat quietly by the phone then looked up at Bryan and said, "I can't believe this is the same plant. This really must be a magic plant."

When Bryan told Pete and Jeannie about his calls, Jeannie very smugly said, "I told you so. I knew it was the same plant."

"What are you going to do with the plant now?" Pete asked.

"I'm thinking about going to Pittsburgh and taking the plant with me. I think I'll take it to the woman who broke it. If she's in the hospital it may give her some comfort to have the plant. Maybe the plant will work its magic for her. Do you have any better ideas?"

"Maybe just one," Pete said slowly. "If Linda, the ballet teacher, left it for someone else, maybe that person needs a turn first."

"But we don't know who that is," Bryan answered.

"But we know where that person lives. Could you take

it there first? If no one is home then you could take it to the hospital," Pete suggested.

Jeannie spoke up. "But we know the lady in the hospital needs it. Hmmm, I just had an idea. I will donate my red geranium for you to take to the hospital in the event you have to leave our original magic plant at the apartment. Maybe my geranium will inherit some good luck charms and bring comfort to the woman."

"That's your plant. I gave it to you," Bryan said.

"And I love it and I want it. But I can't be selfish if it could change someone's life. Anyhow, you can buy me a new one," Jeannie said. "I'll bring it over tonight. You have plenty of room in the van for two red geraniums."

"Don't you just love Jeannie when she gets so bossy?" Pete said in a happy, loving voice.

"And you know what, Bryan? She's usually right."

CHAPTER 10
BRYAN

In spite of Jeannie's protests that he should immediately deliver the magic geranium to the known address, Bryan decided he would take care of it for a few days until he knew that Theresa could have flowers in her room. Every day he nursed the plant. To the untrained eye, no one could tell the plant had been damaged.

A few days later, Bryan got a call from Mrs. Harrington that Theresa would be able to receive the plant. Bryan knew the time had come for him to stop making excuses and go to Pittsburgh. He planned to visit a large warehouse that sold the plants he needed for his rental business. He tried to tell himself he needed to make this trip to purchase the plants. He finally admitted that his mind was only on one type of plant – red geraniums. He knew there was no such thing as real magic. It's all lights and mirrors – scams and nonsense. But he had to admit there was something…

well, something special about this plant that merited the effort of delivering it to its next rightful owner.

Early the next morning he decided to go that day. As he drove along, the memories returned of his trek from Pittsburgh the year before ending in Zanesville. Those memories were slowly fading as each day brought new joy into his life. He admitted he was making this trip because he was obsessed with proper delivery of the red geranium. He had the address and apartment number of the apartment where Linda had lived and he would go there first.

Last night when he had called Mrs. Harrington, she told him that Theresa was in a state of depression. Mrs. Harrington had sounded very worried and grateful that Bryan was willing to make the trip to see Theresa and deliver the red geranium.

It was Bryan's first trip back to the city since he walked away in the icy rain the year before. He was a bit surprised that nothing looked familiar to him. He saw beautiful buildings, busy streets and people who walked with a purpose as if all was well in the world. Bryan had never been able to remember how he even got to Pittsburgh in the first place. *What a waste I made of my life,* he thought, *but I have a good life now.*

Thanks to the van's GPS he easily found the apartment building. He felt a little unsettled as he approached it with the magic red geranium in his hand. He had no idea what he would say. *Would he really be able to give this plant and its story to a stranger?* He rang the main buzzer and announced he had a delivery for a tenant. He was admitted to the office, asked for his business id and directed to the seventh floor. At the door, he knocked, announced "Delivery." *How am I going to explain a red geranium,* he wondered again.

A voice called out, "Just a minute," and he heard a latch turn and the door open.

For a moment there was complete silence as the tenant and Bryan looked at each other.

Then in unison each said the other's name.

"Bryan."

"Katie."

They stood there for a second looking at each other.

Then Katie started to sway.

Bryan quickly set the geranium down and reached out to catch her. He carried her to a chair.

"Put your head between your knees," he quietly but firmly told her. "I'll fix you tea."

Katie said nothing as she sat bent over.

Bryan set the tea kettle on the stove and looked for a tea bag. He felt almost robotic as he went through the motions that suddenly felt very familiar. The last time he had done this was when Katie learned of the sudden death of her beloved grandfather. He knew she now needed a few minutes to collect her thoughts and looked at her while he waited. *She looks just the same as the last time I saw her, before I shipped out to Iraq. No, that's wrong. She is even more beautiful today,* he thought. The whistle of the teakettle roused him from his thoughts. He poured the hot water into the cup, added exactly one level teaspoon of sugar from memory. He carried the cup to her. She lifted her head to look at him.

"Bryan, is it really you?" she asked.

"Yes."

"How did you know I was here?" she asked.

"I didn't know. I was delivering this red geranium to this address."

"A red geranium?"

"It's a long story, but I believe it was meant for you."

"I don't understand." She took a few sips of the hot tea and her color returned. "I need some explanations. You disappear from my life for years and then suddenly appear on my doorstep. Have you been spying on me? How did you know that a red geranium changed my life?" she asked with a raised voice.

Her cell phone rang at that moment. She glanced at the screen impatiently, then spoke a few sentences and ended the call.

"I'm going to be late for court. I have to appear with a client before the judge." She stood up as she spoke. Her eyes closed again and Bryan could see she was unsteady on her feet.

"You're in no condition to drive. Let me take you to the courthouse. I'll wait for you and take you wherever you need to go. Or do you have a husband I can call to take you?"

"No, I never married. The one person I loved left me. I will never let myself feel that way again," she said very sharply.

"Then let's keep this very professional. I'll drive you to court and then drive you home. I will explain about the red geranium and walk out your door." He paused and then quietly said, "I'm so, so sorry I hurt you so badly. Please believe that. But you must not drive right now."

Katie looked a bit subdued and said she'd get her coat. Neither said anything as they made their way to his van. When they arrived at the courthouse, Katie told him she would probably be a half-hour or so. He said he'd wait for her in the little park across the street from the courthouse.

"It may be longer, maybe even an hour before I'm done," she told him.

"I'll wait. No matter how long it takes, I'll wait for you."

Bryan watched her as she walked into the courthouse. *She's the most beautiful woman in the world* he thought. *Why did I treat her so badly? How can I ask for forgiveness? Will she ever be able to understand about my illness? Should I even try?* He sat quietly on the bench and watched some squirrels play in and out of the trees. Bryan felt all the old feelings of the love they shared come over him. *I will not give her up again without first begging, pleading, or doing whatever I can to win her back.*

More than an hour passed. Finally Bryan saw Katie emerge from the building. She was walking with a tall, handsome man. They both were smiling. As they reached the bottom of the courthouse steps, they stopped. The man embraced her and kissed her on the cheek. As he began to walk away he looked back and blew her a kiss. The man couldn't stop smiling.

I have come this far. I don't care who that man is. I will not let Katie leave my life without letting her know I have always loved her. Bryan stood as she neared him. What should he say? What could he do? An old memory flashed through his mind. As soon as she was close to him he reached out his right hand and said, "Hello, my name is Bryan. Would you be interested in going to a lecture tonight on 'The Evolution of the British Flower Gardens' at the lecture hall?"

Just for a moment Katie started to smile. Then very seriously as she shook his hand she said, "Only if you'll let me buy you the best burger in Pittsburgh down at the Box Bar." She looked at him wistfully. "You remembered. You remembered the first time we talked."

"I was so scared to speak to you that first day," he said. "But I can talk now. A burger sounds great."

They began to walk down the street. The Box Bar was a restaurant that was frequented by young attorneys. All the way down the street people greeted Katie. Some were saying "Welcome back." Others were congratulating her on her court appearance that morning with questions including, "How did you hear about her affair?" "Did she sit there and cry to get sympathy?"

"Sounds like you had a successful court appearance. Was it a serious problem?" Bryan asked.

"Not really. The client gave his grandmother's diamond engagement ring to a woman who wouldn't return it when they broke up. We found a man she had been sleeping with while wearing the ring. The judge made her give the ring back. It was my first time in court in more than a year. It was fun to have this case."

As they went through the line to pick up their burgers many people acknowledged Katie.

"You're very popular and much loved," Bryan told her.

"That's because I've only been back a week. I spent the last year traveling in Asia and Australia on a study for the U.N. This was not my case. I was asked to fill in when his attorney had to appear in a different court."

"Then you just came home to Pittsburgh a week ago?" he asked. "I always expected you to practice law in Washington D.C."

"I was a bit upset and jaded about life when I finished law school. I didn't want to practice law. I used the money left me by my grandmother and went to tour Europe for six months. But instead of seeing Europe, I ended up with a relief organization in Africa. When I graduated from law school this firm in Pittsburgh made me an offer and said they'd let me postpone starting for six months. When I got back, I moved here and went to work. After a year I was asked to help in a study for the U.N. for a year. The firm encouraged me to go and kept my job open."

They sat quietly for a minute and then she asked him, "How did you get to Pittsburgh? I thought for sure you'd be in Washington, D.C. or even Maine with your grandmother."

"My grandmother died," he said softly.

"I'm so sorry. You must have been crushed. She was such a sweet, loving lady. She loved you very much. I think she even loved me."

"She told me many, many times how much she loved you. She was a really special woman."

"I'm so, so sorry to hear of her death. But what made you move to Pennsylvania? Are you teaching here? I never imagined you moving to Pittsburgh. Do you have a wife and family?"

"I have no idea how I got to Pittsburgh. And I have no wife or family."

Another group of people came into the restaurant and stopped to speak with Katie. Finally, she looked at Bryan and said, "Let's go to the park. There are too many people here."

As they walked, she turned to him. "What did you mean when you said you didn't know how you got to Pittsburgh?"

Quietly and calmly Bryan began to talk about waking up in an Army Hospital in Germany. Tears filled his eyes as he told her about receiving word of his grandmother's death, and learning it had happened months before he even knew about it. He had had no chance to say goodbye to her. Eventually he was returned to a hospital back in the states.

Finally, he turned to her and said, "I didn't know what to do. Most of the time I didn't even know who I was. It was like I was living in a haze. But I remembered you and how much we loved each other. I felt like I would never be able to live a normal life again. One day someone, I can't remember who, told me I'd better get used to VA Hospitals because I'd probably be living in one for the rest of my life. I knew you were decent and kind. And I knew you loved me. I wanted you to have a better life than I would ever be able to give you. That's when I wrote the letter. And until just recently, I was right. I was in and out of hospitals for the next couple of years and living on the street in between."

They sat quietly. Then Katie's cell phone rang. She answered it saying she'd be there in five minutes.

"I'm running late for a very big meeting. They are waiting to start." She looked at him seriously and then said, "Bryan, you've given me so much to think about. Give me your phone number. I promise I'll call you within a couple of days."

Bryan told her his number and she entered it into her cell phone. As she walked away, he called, "Thank you, Katie, for giving me this chance to see and talk with you. I'll wait for your call."

He watched her walk down the street, and then started to shake all over so badly he sat back down on the bench and buried his head in his hands. He knew beyond all doubt that he still loved her and would always love her. Would he ever be given a chance to tell her that?

Chapter 11
Katie

Katie was shaking all over as she walked away from Bryan. She had tried to appear calm and in control but inside she was torn with emotions: shock at seeing him again, concern for what he had been through without any family or friends to support him, angry with him for the way he cut her out of his life and many other emotions, including most of all, the love she had once felt for this man.

When she got to the corner she looked back and saw him still sitting on the bench in the park, leaning forward with his head buried in his hands. For a moment she yearned to rush back to him and put her arms around him. She had been tempted to ignore the summons for the meeting. But force of habit, and a desire to ensure neither she nor Bryan would be hurt again, took control of her emotions. She continued on her way to the meeting.

She made her apologies for her late arrival and found

a seat at the conference table. But she simply could not concentrate on the discussion. When she heard them ask for a volunteer to travel to California to check some depositions with conflicting information, she volunteered to make the trip. She would be traveling alone and it would give her a chance to clear her head. She knew now that Bryan would forever have her heart.

As the meeting ended, several members of the staff came to congratulate her on her court appearance that morning. She tried to be enthusiastic in response, but inside all she wanted was to be alone, to think about what she should do. Finally the afternoon ended. She got a ride home from the office with a co-worker who lived in the same complex. She hurried into her apartment, fell into a chair and began to cry. She wasn't sure if she was crying because she was happy to know Bryan was okay or angry because this man who appears to be perfectly fine dumped her and then appeared again. She didn't know what to think. She wanted to talk about it with someone. She reached for her phone and dialed her parents.

"Mom, I need to talk to you. Is Dad home?"

"John, get on the line. It's Katie," her mother responded.

"Hi Sweetheart, how did your first day back in court go today? Did you win the case?"

"Hi Daddy, yes, it went well. But something has happened and I need someone to talk to about it."

"You sound serious, Katie," her mother said. "Is something wrong?"

"Well, something happened. I was about ready to leave

for work this morning when my doorbell rang and a voice said 'delivery'. I opened the door and there stood Bryan with a red geranium in his hand. I was so shocked when I saw him all I could do was say his name. I heard him say my name and then I started to faint. He took me to a chair and told me to put my head between my knees. He made me tea. I started to yell at him for trying to surprise me like that but he said he was equally surprised; he had only thought he was making a delivery of a red geranium. He said he would never have tried to surprise me like that; he had only an address and no name for delivery. My phone rang and I realized I was due in court. Bryan said I was in no condition to drive so he drove me to court. He waited for me and we had lunch together and then I had to leave again for a meeting."

"My poor baby," her mother said. "It must have been very shocking to see him there. How in the world did he end up in Pittsburgh? I would have thought he'd return to D.C. or possibly Maine with his grandmother."

"He says he doesn't know how he got to Pittsburgh. He was badly wounded in Iraq and in a hospital in Germany, apparently unconscious, for a time. When he finally started to recover he was told his grandmother had died during his ordeal. He has no other next of kin. He said he has been in and out of VA hospitals since he was wounded and living on the streets in between. He was told at the beginning that he'd probably never fully recover. That's when he wrote me the famous letter. We didn't have time to say much of anything else because I had another meeting. I did find out he isn't married. He said he wanted to talk with me, but I wasn't sure what to do so I said I'd call him. Now I'm going to go to California for a few days. Maybe I can get my head together by the time I get back."

"Did he say how he happened to get your address if there was no name connected with it?" her father asked.

"We really didn't have time to talk. I am so confused I don't know what to do. I loved him so much. You know that, Mom and Dad, but I don't know what to do now."

"He must be suffering from post-traumatic stress. How did he look?" her father asked.

"So handsome that part of me wanted to jump into his arms. He didn't look like a street person. But I don't want to be hurt again either. And I don't know if I can believe anything he says."

Her mother spoke. "He was once a kind, gentle man, respectful of everyone. I'm so sorry to hear he has been on the streets. The shock of losing his grandmother and not being able to say goodbye to her on top of his mental condition probably pushed him over the edge. How did you leave things?"

"I said I'd call him."

"Maybe this is a good time for you to go to California. But before you go or as soon as you come back, do make time to talk with him," her mother urged. "You both need time to talk over what happened when he wrote you that letter. He may have felt pretty desperate at that time. I hope to see you happily married some day with no regrets about the choices you have made. Maybe a few days to think over all that did happened and then a good talk will clear the air and you both can go on to have a happy life. Maybe it will be with each other or maybe you both will find new loves. Do give him our condolences about the death of his grandmother. She was a very, very fine lady."

Chapter 12
Bryan

Bryan sat in the park for a time, trying to absorb what had happened. He wanted to take Katie in his arms and hold her. But her reaction suggested maybe he had lost that chance forever. He may have hurt her too badly to ever be forgiven.

Walking to his van, he noted it was still early in the afternoon. *I must put aside what has happened and concentrate on what I need to get done. I will stop at the warehouse and look at the plants and then go home.* As he got in the van he saw the second red geranium, the one Jeannie had given him as a backup in case he decided to leave the magic plant at the apartment unit. *Well,* he thought, *I guess I will give this plant to Theresa. Maybe it too, will have some magic, in it and help her heal and have a good life.*

When Mrs. Harrington saw Bryan enter Theresa's room, she began to smile. "You fixed it, you fixed it. Look,

look, Theresa, here is the red geranium. It's not broken any more."

Theresa looked up at Bryan from her hospital bed. "You saved my life by bringing me this plant. Can you give it to the woman in the apartment?"

"I took care of that problem all ready. This is a plant for you. And it comes with all my best wishes for you to have a speedy recovery."

Theresa began to smile. Her sister began to weep quietly.

"Red geraniums are very special plants. This could be one of the magic ones that bring nice things to good people. I hope it is one of the magic ones and that it will bring you great happiness," Bryan told her.

Mrs. Harrington left the room with him. "That's probably the first flower anyone has ever given my sister. Thank you and God bless you."

After Bryan had made a stop at the warehouse and purchased twelve new plants, he started to make his way home. He wanted to stay in Pittsburgh so that if Katie called he could be there quickly. But she had said she would call in a couple of days. He'd call her if she didn't call him back. After all, he still wanted to tell her about the magic red geranium he had left on her kitchen counter. He still wanted so badly to hold her in his arms.

The trip home seemed to take forever. Emily had already left and the office was closed. He went to his apartment; then sat in a chair. He didn't feel like eating. He didn't feel like talking. As he sat there meditating, he began to pray. *Lord, you brought me through the darkest nights. I know I don't have any right to ask you but I will anyhow. Please help me to have a second chance with Katie. Help me to heal the hurt I inflected upon her. Help me to help her to be happy again. Amen.*

CHAPTER 13
BRYAN

Bryan got up before five the next morning. There was no sense lying there awake when there was work to be done. He cared for the plants in the greenhouse and pulled to the aisle the plants he would be exchanging today. Then he readied an unused section where he would place the plants he had just purchased in Pittsburgh. He cleaned out another area where he would place the remainder of the poinsettias he had stocked for the Christmas holidays. He did all these things without first having showered and shaved. He had not even made coffee. He heard Emily come in the door.

"Good morning, Bryan. How did yesterday…" She paused when she saw him. "Is something wrong, Bryan? You look like you've been up all night."

"I didn't sleep much."

"Why not go upstairs and get cleaned up? I can take

care of things here for a couple of hours." She gently led him to the back stairwell that led to his apartment.

"Aren't you going to ask me about my trip yesterday?"

"Not yet. You get cleaned up and I'll put on the coffee. I brought some donuts this morning."

When he came back downstairs, he had showered and shaved and put on clean clothes.

"Feeling better?" Emily asked. "Jeannie called already. She wondered how things went yesterday. I told her you would call her back."

Bryan gave her a half smile. "Be honest, Emily. You probably called and told her I was a wreck and she's on her way over here."

"You know me too well. She should be here in about five minutes. You are going to tell us about your trip, aren't you?"

"I may not have much to say."

"Then we'll sit here quietly and have coffee."

As she spoke they saw Jeannie pulling into the parking lot.

Jeannie looked at Bryan, then Emily, then back to Bryan again. "I guess you had a long day yesterday. We waited up to hear from you last night."

"It was late when I made it home," Bryan said quietly.

"I guess it was a hard trip," Jeannie said.

Bryan said nothing.

"Tell us about the red geranium. Did you get to take it to Theresa? How is she doing?"

"I took her the geranium you gave me. She is still not able to leave her room but she seemed very pleased. Her sister cried and told me she thinks it's the first time anyone has ever given Theresa a flower or plant. She is sure that Theresa will be encouraged by it."

"Did you tell her it was a magic plant?" Emily asked.

"No, but I did tell her that sometimes red geraniums are magic and I hoped this one would bring her happiness."

"What about the magic geranium?" Jeannie asked.

"I delivered it to the apartment," Bryan said quietly.

"Was the person there surprised? Pleased?"

"The door to the apartment was opened by Katie."

"Katie?" Jeannie paused before remembering. "Your Katie from years ago?" Jeannie asked.

"Yes, that Katie."

"I have to sit down," Jeannie said. "I thought she lived in Washington, D.C. Did you recognize each other instantly? What happened?"

"Yes, we recognized each other instantly. Then she started to faint. I sat her down, made her tea, and drove her to court. She's an attorney in Pittsburgh. I waited for her. We had lunch together and then she had to go back to work."

"Did you talk at all about your past together? Is she married? Are you going to see her again?"

"We talked a little. She is not married 'because some jerk dumped her and she will never let anyone get close to her again'. She asked for time to think. She said she'd call me."

Emily asked, "What about the red geranium? Did she seem surprised by it? Did she want to keep it?"

"We had no chance to talk about it. I set it down when

she started to faint. I seem to remember she said something about a red geranium but I don't remember what she said. Then she was occupied with her work day."

"It's a first step, Bryan. You can't expect her to jump into your arms after you dumped her. She needs some time," Jeannie said.

"But you must tell her about the history of the red geranium. Don't let her go until you have told her," Emily added.

"I may not have the chance. But I'm feeling better after the coffee and donut. Let me tell you about the new plants I bought. And I have a new idea for picking up the holiday sales. I need your expert opinion."

Knowing Bryan had closed the subject, the women looked at each other and allowed him to shift the conversation.

Somehow Bryan made it through the day and decided to go to bed around nine o'clock to make up for his lack of sleep the night before. About ten thirty his phone rang.

"It's Katie. Am I calling too late?"

Bryan was instantly awake. "It's not too late. Did you have a busy day today?"

"It was pretty hectic. I didn't get much done yesterday."

There was a pause on the line. Then Bryan asked, "How are your parents and brothers?"

"The boys are both married. Chuck is in New York working in criminal law, and Jack is in California with a corporate law firm. Dad and Mom are still teaching, consulting, and taking occasional cases. I told them I talked with you."

"They must hate me for what I did to you."

"They don't hate you. They were sorry to hear about your grandmother and sorry you have had such a hard life. I didn't know what to tell them about your life today. Where do you live? Did you continue your plan to teach? I know it was your passion for a time."

"I lived on the streets for a few years. In between times, my home was in one VA hospital or another. One day I found a red geranium plant. It seemed to appear out of nowhere. I picked it up and walked away from the streets that night and ended up about seventy miles from Pittsburgh. A very nice man and woman took me into their home. With their help I turned my life around. That was more than a year ago. Now I have my own business. People call me a plant doctor. I rent out plants to businesses and take care of ailing plants. It's not the big landscaping nursery, or the teaching career I hoped to have, but I'm doing okay. I'm already making plans to expand my business in the spring."

The phone line was quiet for a minute. Then Katie spoke.

"I'm really, really sorry to hear how you lived, but you must be doing okay. Where are you living now, Bryan? Were you married? Do you have kids? How did you get into the flower business?"

"I live in Zanesville. It's about seventy miles from Pittsburgh. My first job was in a grocery store. I had some dealings with fresh flowers. It awakened in me my love for the beauty of nature. One thing led to another and I went to work for a man who sold me his business. I live upstairs over the shop. I named the shop 'The Red Geranium'. I never married and I have no kids. What about you? You said you never married because some jerk of a guy dumped you. Do you have anyone special in your life right now? Do you have any kids?"

"No to both questions. I think I told you I just got back in town."

"It was good to see you did get your law degree."

"I almost quit law school after I got your letter. There were memories of you everywhere. Then, when I received an offer for a job here in Pittsburgh, I thought a change of scenery away from D.C. would be best for me. I loved the work I did in Africa after I graduated, and had I not already signed the contract to come to Pittsburgh, I might have stayed there. But because of the contract, I did come back. Then I got a request from the U.N. to help on a project. Now I'm back in Pittsburgh to finish out my contract."

"They're lucky to have you back."

"Well, they are already keeping me busy. I have to go to California tomorrow morning. I might be gone as long as a week."

"Would it be okay to call you there?"

The line went silent. Then Katie spoke quietly. "Bryan, I'm not sure it's the best thing to do."

"Katie, I never meant to cause you pain. I am so, so sorry I hurt you."

"I have never been as surprised in my life as when I saw you at my door."

"I was equally surprised, Katie. Had I known you lived there I might have tried a different way to deliver the red geranium."

"I never did hear why you brought it to me."

"It's a long story. Do you think we could meet one more time when you get back from your trip? I'm not asking for any commitment from you. Perhaps we could meet one more time to say goodbye."

"Maybe that would be a good idea. I'll be honest with you, Bryan. In the last twenty-four hours I have gone from being surprised to see you, to being happy to see you, to being very angry with you, and yes, even wanting to see you again. Maybe my trip will give me time to sort things out." She paused for a minute and then said, "I'll give you my cell number. But I'll call you."

"I'll wait for your call. And if some night you can't sleep and feel lonely, give me a call."

"You'd hate me. Think of the time difference."

"Who cares about that?" Bryan said. "I'll wait to hear from you."

Bryan wondered if maybe there was just a sliver of reason to hope in her voice. *Probably not,* he thought, *but I won't give up yet. We still have to talk about the red geranium.*

Chapter 14
The Red Geranium

A few days later, Bryan woke up around three in the morning. Remembering the slow if growing warmth of his last conversation with Katie, he reached for his cell phone and hit the send button by Katie's number. "Is it too late to talk?" he asked as she answered the phone.

"I was just getting into bed. I'm glad you called," she said softly.

"Did you have a hard day today?"

"It was a tiring day. That's probably because I'm not yet back into the routine I usually follow. But I'm okay. How did your day go?"

"Well, I did rounds of the locations where I place fresh-cut flowers for sale and brought back the tired ones. I talked with a vendor about spring supplies. And I did a final inventory of the Christmas items I have for sale. Nothing very exciting. I did grab a burger for lunch. It wasn't as good as the burger at the Box Bar. Hmmm, maybe it was because you were there that that made that burger the best."

"What was the name of the place where we used to get burgers in D.C? Oh, I remember. It was Johnny's or something like that, wasn't it? They were really good."

They chatted for about five minutes and then Bryan told her he'd let her get some sleep.

It's a start. If I hope to have a life with Katie I'll have to be patient. But I'll do it. I'll even get on my knees if I have to.

The week passed slowly for Bryan. Things at the Red Geranium kept him busy. His Christmas items were selling well. He was getting multiple visits from sales reps who wanted him to sell their wares in the early spring. Some items seemed like a good investment. But if he decided to carry them, it meant that he had to make more space for inventory. He began to plan how to expand both his indoor and outdoor space.

In most ways he was a happy man. Not only was he off to a good start with his new business, his clients were paying promptly, and he continued to get new customers from as far as forty miles away seeking to rent decorative live plants for business use and personal events. He was happy because he had Pete and Jeannie who were always supporting and encouraging him. But most of all, he was happy because he had one more chance to see Katie again. They had only missed one day of talking to each other. Mostly it was just chitchat about their day. But it was a beginning.

Late on Saturday night his phone rang. It was Katie calling to say she had just finished up the business in

California and was at the airport waiting to return to Pittsburgh.

"Would you like me to meet you at the airport?" he asked her.

"That would be crazy for you to drive seventy-five miles to drive ten miles to my home. I can grab a cab that'll have me home in twenty minutes or so."

"It would give me great pleasure to do it."

"I'm expecting to get in around five or six in the morning. Why don't I take a cab home and grab some sleep." She was quiet for a moment and then asked, "Would it be too far for you to come for an early dinner?"

"It's not too far, but don't cook. Let me take you to your favorite restaurant."

"Okay," she said, and then continued, "Bryan, we both have changed over the years. Maybe we've changed too much to ever capture what we had before." She spoke quietly and calmly. "We did have something special. I have never loved any man but you. Do you think we could meet as friends and try to see if our time apart has really separated us forever? Maybe it's not too late for us to see where our friendship might take us."

"I hope it's not too late. I never stopped loving you. I never did. I don't feel worthy of your love. I treated you so badly. Can you ever forgive me for sending you that letter and then disappearing from your life? As much as I want you in my life now, I know I need to earn your trust. It will make me happy to have you as my friend again."

"Does that mean dinner is on for tomorrow?"

"It certainly does. Come home, get some sleep and call

me as soon as you wake up. It'll take me over an hour to get to your place so you'll have time for a cup of coffee before I get there. I do love you, Katie."

"Goodnight, Bryan. I'll call you in a few hours."

Bryan slept well that night. In the morning he thought of nothing but Katie. He went through his thousandth period of angst as he realized how much he had hurt her. He had never, ever, heard Katie talk with the tone of voice she used when she first saw him. He should have given her a chance to dump him. Why, oh why, had he been so cruel?

Waiting for the phone to ring so he could start on his way to see her, he heard his doorbell. Seeing Jeannie and Pete through the window, he pushed the buzzer to let them in.

"Good morning, Bryan. Hope we didn't wake you. We're skipping church today to go see one of Jeannie's cousins. We didn't want you to worry about us."

"As a matter of fact, Pete, I'm skipping church too. Katie was due back in Pittsburgh around five or six this morning. She's going to get a couple of hours sleep and call me. I'm going to take her to dinner."

"Are you two friends yet?" Jeannie asked.

"I think so. At least I hope so"

"Well, well. I'm glad to hear that. I brought this apple pie with me to give you. I had baked it for dinner today but I don't want to take it with me. Take this pie with you. Maybe it will remind you never to give up hope. I think Katie needs some time. If she hated you or had someone else in her life, I don't believe she would agree to see you again."

"Don't forget to tell her about the red geranium," Pete said.

After they left, Bryan thought about the plant still in Katie's possession.

"Did you work your magic on her, Red Geranium?" he wondered.

Bryan put on a pair of dress slacks and his best sweater. He knew Katie hated fancy restaurants and much preferred places where they could be very casual. He decided to change into his jeans and wear his leather jacket. He was in the car and on his way two minutes after Katie called to tell him she was awake.

Katie looked gorgeous. Her light brown hair, which had been in a bun on the back of her head when working, was hanging in a ponytail, tied with a blue ribbon. She had on a blue and white striped shirt and her jeans. Bryan heaved a sigh of relief that he had also worn jeans.

"Here. This pie is for our dessert tonight." Bryan put it on the counter next to the red geranium.

"Don't tell me you made it."

"You know me better than that. Jeannie made it for dinner today, but they had to go out of town so she brought it to me."

"We can come back here for dessert and coffee."

"Do you have a favorite restaurant?" he asked.

"We have all kinds right here in the neighborhood. What would you like?"

"Why don't you choose some place for us? You know them better than I."

"I have a favorite Italian restaurant just down the block. I haven't had time to go there since I've been back, but the food was always great before. Does that sound okay?"

"It sounds good to me."

Together they walked to the restaurant where Katie was welcomed back by the owner. The wait staff hovered, giving them great service. After the meal, Bryan and Katie left the restaurant to walk back to her apartment. Though it was mid-December, the afternoon sun was bright in the cool, crisp air.

"It's a beautiful day," Katie smiled. "I really missed this city when I was gone. I was lucky enough to get my old office back after my year away. The view from my office window is of the two rivers merging into the Ohio River. I love looking at the scene. The Ohio River seems to mean a new beginning to me."

"I'd love to see it sometime," Bryan told her. "Now I know what it feels like to dine with a celebrity. The staff certainly gave you a warm welcome."

"Aren't they just the sweetest people?" she said. "They have been so good to me."

At her apartment, Bryan said, "Tell me about your trip to the coast. Did you accomplish everything?"

"Well, the trip was prep work for an upcoming trial. I interviewed quite a few people about the depositions they had given. Actually, it was very routine. Not the most interesting work, but it needed to be done."

"Did you get a chance to see your brother?"

"I sure did. We had dinner one night. Jack said to tell you hello."

"You make me cringe when you say that. He must hate me for what I did to his little sister."

"Bryan, my family doesn't hold grudges. My folks have always told me to look ahead and not look back." She went to the kitchen. "I think the coffee's done now. Are you ready for some pie with it?"

"Jeannie does make good pies. She had made an apple pie the first time I saw her."

"She must be a special lady."

"She is. Even though she was deep in grief over the loss of her son in Iraq, and I was a dirty, stinking derelict with filthy clothes, a long beard and long dirty hair, she welcomed me into her home. She told me to take a shower and shave, gave me clean clothes and a haircut and a bed to sleep in. Not too many people do that."

"Is it too hard to talk about?" Katie asked. "You mentioned something about the red geranium."

"It started with the red geranium that's on your kitchen counter. The one I was asked to deliver to this apartment. It was more than a year ago now that I woke up one cold, rainy night and found the geranium by my side. Somewhere deep in my psyche it did remind me of my grandmother and her hopes for me. I couldn't get back to sleep. I walked away from my so-called home that night, carrying the red geranium. I didn't know where I was going but I walked and walked and walked. I slept in doorways and ate from garbage cans. By the third day I had no idea where I was, but I knew I had to have real food or I would probably collapse and die. A truck driver gave me a ride to Pete's Grocery Store in Zanesville and told me to go trade the plant for a sandwich. Pete agreed to the trade but didn't stop there. He took me home with him. We took the geranium with us and gave it to Jeannie. He told me I could pay for my food and lodging by working in his grocery store and letting his wife fuss over me. Pete and Jeannie had not been living a normal life since they heard of the death of their son. Jeannie was a hair stylist who closed her shop and her life when she learned of Joe's death. She actually cut my long hair for me in her shop, which she had closed the day she got the bad news. Jeannie and I helped each other. But all of us credited the red geranium with being the good luck charm that brought us back to the land of the living."

"Then you've had the plant all this time. How did my name or address get involved?" she asked.

"This may be hard to believe, but I swear it is true. A year ago on Thanksgiving Day, Pete and Jeannie invited me for dinner along with a little old lady who lived at the top of the mountain. Alma had no friends or family. She did have a daughter who lived in Scranton, but they were estranged from one another. Jeannie gave her the red geranium since she thought it should be passed along so that others could have nice things happen to them. The plant did its job for Alma. Alma reconciled with her daughter and has moved to be close to her.

"Alma planned to take the plant with her but accidentally left it behind. It was found by a couple from Philadelphia hiking in the area. They rescued the plant and brought it to Pete because they were interested in buying Alma's house. He told them to keep the plant. Turns out they were successful professionally, but not happy about some problems at work for him and a desire to have a baby for both of them. Within a few short weeks after getting the geranium, he was given a promotion at work and she became pregnant.

"That woman gave the geranium to a woman she had worked with who had lost her job. After that woman got the plant, she got a job knitting special-order sweaters and managing a yarn shop. She is very, very, happy and successful professionally.

"That woman passed it on to the man who owned the yarn shop. He was a man of about seventy years who had existed, not lived, since his wife had died. She hoped he would find some happiness in his personal life. Apparently a long-time female friend came back to town and pulled him back into the world of the living, including dance lessons.

"He gave the plant to the couple who ran the dance studio. They were having a lot of financial problems but both got new jobs after receiving the plant. The woman is now the new Dance Master at the School for the Arts here in Pittsburgh. She brought the plant with her. She lived here in your apartment for two weeks while their condo was being painted. When she left the apartment, she decided the plant had been so good for her and her husband that she should leave it for the next person who would live here. That was you."

"My goodness, it hardly seems possible for all that to

happen," Katie said. "But how did you get it back again in Zanesville?"

"In cleaning your apartment before your return, the cleaning lady, Theresa, knocked the plant off the counter and broke a branch."

"I know Theresa. She's a sweetheart. She's always so kind and sweet," Katie said. "But I haven't seen her since I've been back."

"That's because she's in the hospital. She was so very upset about the accident that an old illness recurred. Apparently she was afraid she'd lose her job because she broke the branch. Her sister lives in Zanesville and brought it to me. I was able to repair the plant and offered to deliver it for Theresa to this address so that management would never know she broke it."

They both sat quietly and pondered the story. Then Katie asked him to tell her how he'd traced the plant, and why.

He told her of his phone conversations. Then he said, "You asked me why. I can't honestly answer you. Everyone who had this plant found happiness. Since the last tenant of this apartment wanted you to have it, even though she didn't know you, Pete, Jeannie and I decided I should bring it to the person who lived here – you."

Katie carried the plant to the coffee table and sat down on the floor so she could touch it. Quietly she said, "And it did bring me happiness. I got to see you again."

Bryan moved to the floor to sit beside her. He put his arms around her. They sat that way for a few minutes, neither saying anything.

Then Katie said, "I don't know much about flowers. You taught me what I do know when you also taught me about trees, stars, and everything else there is to know about nature. My courses in school were always about law. But I, too, have a tale about a magic red geranium.

"Right after I came to work at the law firm here in Pittsburgh, one of our senior attorneys had family friends who had lost all their money. He asked me to look into the cause. I did so and we uncovered a massive fraud case. Because I had so much paperwork, I was given an office that was being vacated. The day I moved in, the man who was moving out gave me a red geranium. He said it had been given to him when he moved into the office. He was told it would bring him good luck. It did do that. He was promoted to V.P. and got a bigger office. He said he was sure the plant would also bring me good luck. And it did. We not only got a good settlement for the old couple, but we closed down a fraudulent medical clinic and phony bank. So I have my own good-luck story about red geraniums."

"What happened to it?" Bryan asked.

"Actually, I tried to pass it on when I left for the U.N. But the person I tried to give it to didn't want it. He said to throw it out. I couldn't do that. I brought it home with me. I was leaving the next morning for New York. I ended up taking it with me when I took some sandwiches and cookies to some homeless people living under the highway near here. I thought that maybe someone living there could use some good luck…"

Katie stopped abruptly. "Bryan," she said, "Look at me. Look at me."

Bryan's eyes were closed and his body had begun to tremble.

"Bryan, look at me." Her voice got louder. "Open your eyes and look at me. Do you have some medication you should take? Bryan, I'm frightened. Tell me what to do to help you."

Bryan reached out to take her hand. Very quietly he said, "I'll be okay now. I'll be okay." He paused for a moment, then said, "Katie, I was the person who was lying under the overpass on the ground. You left this plant by my side. Katie, you saved my life."

"That can't be. How would I not know it was you? Surely I would have known." She was talking rapidly and loud, in a voice full of tears.

"You had no way to know it was me, Katie. I was so far gone you had no way to know it was me. Tell me, Katie, did you bring anything else besides the plant and sandwiches?"

"I think so. Yes, I brought cookies, apples, and water."

"And you also brought one other thing," Bryan began. "You brought hot coffee…"

"…in my big red thermos bottle."

"I have that red thermos now, at home. I saved it to remind me to never let myself go back to that life again. Now I know why that geranium was magic. It was your spirit and your love that saved me."

They clung to each other tearfully.

Finally, Katie spoke very quietly. "I don't know why I felt such an attachment to a plant. But I did. I can remember I even wrote a note, wrapped it in foil and stuck it in the plant. I can't remember exactly what I said but it was something like 'This is a magic plant…'"

"…It will bring you good luck. Take care of it." Bryan finished the sentence for her and reached for his wallet. He removed the note that he had taken from the plant when he re-potted it.

"That's the note I wrote." Katie began to cry again. "How could I not have known it was you?"

"Maybe because the good Lord knew I needed time to heal before I saw you again."

They sat quietly with their arms wrapped around each other. Then Katie softly said, "Because I'm responsible for saving your life once, does it mean I'm responsible for your happiness for the rest of our lives?"

Bryan started to smile. "Who but you would think of the perfect way to say something? I'm sure that's what it means. Will you take on that job?"

"Yes, Bryan. I want that job for the rest of my life," she said as she pressed her lips against his.

They both looked at the red geranium. They could have sworn it was smiling.